Don't Stop

Lauren Biel

Library of Congress Cataloging-in-Publication Data

Don't Stop/Lauren Biel 1st ed.

Cover Design: Pretty in Ink

Editing: Sugar Free Editing

Interior Design: Sugar Free Editing

For more information on this book and the author, visit: www. LaurenBiel.com

Please visit LaurenBiel.com for a full list of content warnings.

This is for my readers who are brave enough for a mix of dark humor, spice, Frankenpeens, and corpse threesomes. Ride or die! Well . . . ride AND die.

Chapter One

Dalton

A bird hits my windshield, and blood splatters across the glass. Black feathers cling to the blood, each one streaked with a deep blue-green hue that reminds me of water poisoned by an oil slick. It's like the poor creature exploded on impact, leaving nothing but his feathers and a smear of crimson behind.

"Fuck," I say.

I feel bad for the thing, but come the fuck on. I just washed this piece-of-trash car.

The wiper blade crosses in front of my face, but it only succeeds in painting an arc of red across the glass. Windshield cleaner jets toward the mess and gets most of it off before I crash and end up a bloody splatter myself. I grab a napkin stuffed into one of the cup holders and lower the window so I can struggle to remove what the wiper blade missed. How did so much blood come from such a small body? I shift in my seat at the thought.

When I pull the blood-soaked napkin back into the car,

I look at it for a moment before bringing it to my nose. It smells like metal with a hint of chemicals from the wiper fluid. I brush my thumb through the red smear, then I bring the painted skin toward my mouth. It tastes how it smells. Chemical-infused death.

See, I like the sight and smell of blood—the life force within the veins of all things living—but I really love to taste it.

My long-dead mother's judgmental fingers grip and squeeze my spine as I ball up the napkin and throw it into the cup holder. She used to scold me whenever I licked my own cuts. Then I'd asked to lick hers, and she beat my ass for it. Called me a freak.

I'm not a freak. I'm just different.

To be clear, I never hurt things to get my fix, even if I sometimes fantasized about it. I just wanted to taste the aftermath of what had already happened. The blood was going to flow whether I touched it to my tongue or left it alone.

If my mother was alive, she'd see that I figured my shit out. Kinda. I'm a professional painter, which sounds boring, but it soothes my anxiety. It also sends my obsessive tendencies into overdrive, and those tendencies make me *very* good at my job. I have my own apartment, I make a decent living, and I'm fairly content. But maybe not entirely content. At twenty-four, I've never had a tangible relationship, and my mother's words still taunt me whenever I try to talk to any woman.

Freak.

Loser.

Weirdo.

She did quite the number on my self-esteem and psyche, but it's fine. I'm doing fucking great.

Aside from the bloody tissue beckoning me from the cup holder, that is.

A pang in my bladder reminds me that I have to pee—a gnawing urge that's plagued me for the last two hours. I should have gone while I was at my last job, but I hate using people's bathrooms. It's fucking weird. It's awkward to ask and awkward for them to answer. Just. Weird. I think I'd rather piss my pants than get their attention and ask to use their bathroom.

Warmth burns my lower lip, and I move my tongue toward the heat. That's the thing about blood for me. It doesn't actually warm me, but psychologically, it lights anywhere it touches me on fire.

My reflection catches my attention. The busted visor hangs in a permanent open position. My car is a piece of shit, I know that, but at least it started this time. It's on my list of things to upgrade, I swear. My tongue swipes across my lower lip once more before I raise my eyes to meet my reflection and ensure I've gotten all of it. A chunk of dark hair falls forward and covers one of my gray eyes. Women are always struck by the intensity of their color. My looks aren't what turn women away from me.

I wish I was as ugly as I feel on the inside. It would make things a lot easier. I wouldn't have to exist in a world where people pay attention to me until I talk or do something fucking weird. I'm sick of seeing the smile slowly dissipate as I open my mouth. Disappointment is such an expressive emotion. It's hard to miss. I've been seeing that look on people's faces for as long as I can remember.

Aside from my mother's constant chagrin, my earliest memory of disgusting the opposite sex happened in elementary school. A girl in my class wanted to be my girlfriend . . . until I gave her a dead frog I found in a puddle before I got on the bus. I'd kept it in my pocket because I wanted to look at it later when I had time, and I figured she'd be just as intrigued as I was. She was not.

What can I say? I've never been good with the ladies.

But it doesn't mean I don't deserve someone who can appreciate me in all my weird, fucked-up glory.

I fidget with the hem of my sweater sleeve and pick at flakes of dried white paint that cling to the threads. Anxiety courses through me. I'm not just a lonely blue-collar worker. I'm a weird one with a blood fetish too. One just contributes to the other. What a lucky draw. If I were a billionaire with some weird fetish, I wouldn't have any issues finding a partner, but because I'm very firmly planted in the lower-to-middle class, I'm a freak. A weirdo.

One day I'll meet a woman who isn't ripped in half by equal parts attraction and disgust when she gets to know me. She will be *different* like me. Or not like me. But still different. Once I find the puzzle piece that fits so well with my own, all this self-loathing will take a back seat to love. Loving myself. Loving someone else.

Unless I'm destined to be the isolated middle piece, sitting idle in the center of an abandoned attempt at a puzzle. At this point, it could go either way. And I'm not expecting it to change anytime soon.

Rayna

TAPE RUBS AGAINST MY WRISTS, and my flesh burns as I move my hands to try to create space within the bindings. My eyes keep darting to the man in the driver's seat in front of me. I can barely hear the music on the radio over my thumping heartbeat in my head. My hands' sawing motions move in time with the song, and soon my skin feels like it's ripping off with every pass. The increasing amount of give makes it all worth it, though. If I don't get out of this bind, he'll hurt me much worse than this. I've seen his face. He won't let the hitchhiker he picked up and assaulted live a life where she can tell on him. I'm a liability.

My eyes move to the dash clock, and I work faster. I'm probably about to be murdered, but I'm just as concerned with my 9:30 p.m. curfew at the sober living home I'm assigned to. I can't miss that fucking curfew because I've thrown my sobriety out the window tonight, and that's how I've ended up raped and in some psychotic dad's car.

I'm pretty sure he thinks I'm unconscious. He hasn't looked back at me once. Rookie mistake. I was almost unconscious, but I'm very much awake now. Dealing with the burn between my legs and the ache on the right side of my head from where he hit me with the flashlight almost makes me wish I was still out. The blood has congealed, and the cold stickiness itches. I focus on that itchiness as I rub my skin raw beneath the tape.

This isn't the first time I've been assaulted. Or the last time, I'm sure. I love putting myself in situations that only my vagina can get me out of, I guess. I'd love it if more women stopped when they spotted me on the side of the road with my thumb in the wind, but it's usually the men. Women tend to fear hitchhikers, even females, or are too distracted by a baby in the backseat to notice me. The men either intend on assaulting me or are actually concerned. I wish more were the latter. Unfortunately, I got into the car with the former this time, and I need to get out before it's the last car I ever get into.

Shielded by the darkness, I lean over and bring the tape to my mouth, gnawing like a little rabbit trapped in a snare. That's exactly what I am. I'm about an exit away from getting slaughtered, and I refuse to resign myself to that fate. I've taken too many steps through hell to let this disturbed dipshit send me there permanently.

My tooth slices through a piece of the tape, and I slam my eyes close and pray as soon as the sound reaches my ears. If there is a god, I hope he finds sympathy for me, even if I've done little to deserve it.

The driver doesn't turn around—he didn't hear the ripping sound over his shit music—and I breathe a silent sigh of relief. I finally pry my hands apart and unlock the door, staying as quiet and still as I can. When I grip the handle, I take a deep breath before pushing open the door and leaping onto the highway. Getting hit by a car is a very real possibility, but it's a risk I'm willing to take because it's most definitely better than a slow murder by bludgeoning or strangling from the fat piece of shit in the driver's seat.

My body slams against the pavement, and the wind evacuates my lungs. A silent scream rises from my chest and evaporates into the night air. His headlights dart as he swerves when he realizes I've escaped his disgusting grasp. The lights flash and glare off the dark pavement as he tries to turn around. The pain in my bones ripples through my body, but I have no time to live in anguish. If I don't get up, I'll get hit by traffic or he'll come back around for me. Those wild lights drift closer to stare at me dead on.

I will my body to move. I force it with intrusive thoughts about my homicide. *Get up, bitch. Go. He's going to kill the fuck out of you.*

I struggle to my knees, and my jeans rip where they scraped the pavement. Everything hurts. Despite my limp, I allow the bolts of adrenaline to fuel my steps, urging me into a light jog toward a nearby guardrail. I push myself over it, then I seek out the safety of the trees along the highway. Branches attack me as I intrude on their serenity. My throat strains as I fight back cries of pain because I don't want him to hear me. My heartbeat hurts my ears, a thunderous sound that rattles me to my core.

The very same flashlight he bludgeoned me with now breaks through the darkness and spreads light along the tree trunks. I dive to the ground, my fingers digging into the soil as I clutch at nothingness for safety. The light makes a few passes nearby before it turns off, but I don't dare move. He's probably listening. Waiting for any sound to tell him to keep going. To keep searching for me.

I stay on the ground for as long as I can. Soil and blood cake my brown hair. The bloodstained locks look nearly black as they stick to my sweat-soaked cheeks. Even they hurt. I roll onto my back and inhale sharp breaths as my adrenaline wanes and the pain mauls me. It feels like I'm being pressed into the ground by a monstrous weight. I groan because I can't go to the hospital. I *have* to get back to Somerset House. I'll just have to nurse my wounds myself, like I've done so many times before. Despite how horrible it can be on my own, it's still better than relying on someone else. Even if I don't give myself the best advice. Or the best care. Hurting myself is better than allowing someone else to hurt me, though.

This sucks, but I'll walk it off because I have one hour to get back to the sober living facility before I'm locked out for good. And that would mean returning to jail. So yeah, walk it off, bitch.

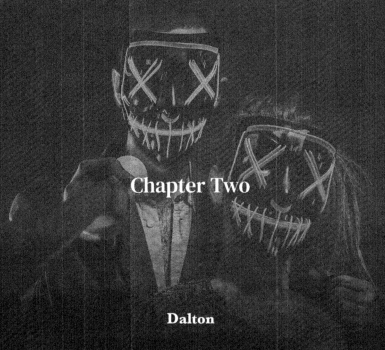

Chapter Two

Dalton

The smell of someone's dinner fills the air and makes my stomach growl. The hearty scent overpowers the chemical odor of the paint I've used on the walls. It smells like chicken and dumplings. My mother used to make it, and it was my favorite meal. But that was before she realized how much she despised my very being and stopped making anything I enjoyed.

I ignore the rumble of starvation and the painful memories of my childhood as I slide the blue paint-coated roller along the wall to smooth out a streak of lines I've spotted. I drown my insecurities in the paint can in front of me as I stare at the seam of my very last stroke. My OCD sucks sometimes, and I've overstayed my welcome, but the wall is nearly perfect. With one final pass of the roller, I dissolve the last visible seam. It's finally acceptable to me.

"Are we all set, Mr. Andrews?" the homeowner asks with an annoyed snip in her tone.

Fuck you, I want to say. *Do you want a nice fucking*

room or what? But I bite my tongue. I won't get more business by letting that monstrous side of me out to give his best fuck-you.

"Yup," I say as I drop the roller into the pan. It splatters up and marks my sweater with a new splash of blue. They had their air conditioner blasting Arctic winds inside, and I'm glad I had my sweater. Painting with a shivering hand never comes out well. I've had to cancel jobs before because of it. Now I always bring a sweater and an undershirt in my bag in case it's too hot or too cold in these houses.

Her eyes rise to meet mine. The smile on her face falls, and so does my gaze. The searing heat of her renewed judgment singes my skin as I pack up my shit, throw the backpack straps over my shoulders, and walk past her. Her laser-beam eyes burn a hole through the back of my sweater.

"Hey," she says, and I stop once my hand grips the door handle. There's an insufferable amount of silence as I wait for her to continue. "Never mind," she says.

I close my eyes for a moment because she probably wanted to thank me. Or tell me I'm unpleasant, which has happened. Thank God I'm my own boss or I'd be fired for my award-winning personality. Like a perfect customer-service-oriented employee with an antisocial personality, I leave without saying another word. I'm tired now. The little bit of pleasantry I can force out of myself is already unconscious. The obsessive compulsion to do things perfectly has worked my body ragged, and I wish I could just curl up and go to sleep. But no, I have to drive home.

I leave the house and step into the night air. The temperature ticks lower as the calendar marches toward one of my favorite holidays—Halloween. I don't go trick-or-treating or anything, but the horror-filled scary movies I love are perfectly acceptable to watch this time of year.

Don't Stop

I shrug off the sweater stained with an array of colors that never come out no matter how many times I wash it, and I open my car door. I don't want to get the fresh paint on anything else, so I turn the sweater inside out and ball it up before tossing it into the backseat. When I flop into the seat, I can only think of getting home and crawling into my bed, where I no longer have to interact with anyone.

My eyelids droop as I drive the familiar stretch of highway. The tires roll over each seam in the pavement and produce rhythmic road noise. It's like a lullaby. I rub the bridge of my nose and lower the window to let the loud roar of wind wake me up. Even then, my eyes still fight me.

A shape takes form on the side of the road. It looks like a person, but I'm tired enough that I could be imagining it. A pale thumb hangs in the air, and hair as dark as the night blows from beneath her hood. At least, I *think* it's a her.

What the fuck is a girl doing out here, hitchhiking like this?

I drive just past the girl and pull onto the shoulder. My head whips backward as I look behind me to see if she's coming toward my car. She hesitates before taking uneven steps toward me, as if she's hurt.

The sight brings me back to a childhood memory of a time I found a cat limping along the side of the road. I was too young to do anything about it, but my curiosity begged me to follow it. The thing stopped, fell, and by the time I reached it, it had died. My mom thought I killed it, so she beat me with a belt until I had welts. I would never kill an animal.

I look at the dried bloodstains on the napkin beside me and swallow.

I would never kill an animal *intentionally*. But I've had fantasies about killing people plenty. She couldn't beat that out of me. Sometimes even now, I imagine putting one of my irritating clients between the steps in my ladder and slamming it shut, breaking their neck in the mash of metal. Other times I envision painting the walls with someone's blood instead of paint—perfect, even strokes of strong crimson.

A faraway voice barges into my sick, dark fantasy. It grows closer. "Hello?" she says.

Her gray eyes remind me of mine, but hers have a bit more blue in them. She looks like she's been beaten up. A cut runs through her swollen lower lip, and her nails are dirty. She has a bit of blood in her dark hair as well. She looks me up and down as much as I'm scanning her, and a weird silence spreads between us.

I should drive the fuck off. What am I even doing? I don't stop to talk to people I get paid to talk to.

"H-Hi . . ." I say.

"I need a ride to Somerset House," she says. Her tone is very matter of fact, but I'm not sure of the fact at all.

I don't know what the fuck compels me to do it, but I nod. Her hand grazes the window frame before she walks around the front of my car and tries to open the passenger-side door. She jiggles the handle, and I snap out of my confused daze enough to hit the unlock button so she can get into my car.

My personal space.

The moment she sits down, the aroma of dirt reaches my nose. It's similar to the lingering smell of a wet dog after it dries. A metallic scent encircles me and makes me dizzy with a drunkenness I can't explain. As if she just intoxicated me with her very presence. Her blood perfume. I don't like it. It calls to a part of myself I can't control.

Beneath the car's dome light, I can see the extent of her

injuries, and I realize why the blood smell is so rampant. A gash runs along the side of her head, and a dried streak of dark red drips toward her cheek. Her knees are scraped raw. The palms of her hands are bloody. What the fuck happened to this girl? And why isn't she more upset about it?

She's fucking weird.

And now this weirdo is in my car.

Without saying anything further—I'm too busy bathing in her intoxicating scent to think—I pull away from the shoulder and head the way I was going. Back toward home.

"It's the next exit, to the right," she says before settling into the seat beside me. At least she can get comfortable, I guess. For me, every muscle strains against my bones, tensing and tightening. She rubs her sore hands down the front of her jeans. "The silent ones make me more uncomfortable than the talkative ones," she whispers.

"Ones?"

"Men."

"Ah, sorry. I'm not a big talker." That's an understatement. I avoid talking at any opportunity I can. You learn more about people by listening. Instead of worrying about engaging conversationally, I study her body language. Like the way she rubs her thumbnail against her jeans, making a scratching sound with every pass, or how she rolls her lower lip between her teeth as she actively avoids looking at me.

"What's your name?" she asks.

Fuck you. That's what my name is.

Her thumb motions speed up, and it's like she's dragging her nail over my last remaining nerve instead of her pants.

"If I tell you my name, will you stop what you're doing with your thumb? Please?"

Instead of stopping, she increases the speed until the sound grows intolerable.

I consider lying, but I will never meet this girl again in my life. Hopefully. Plus, I've never been a very good liar. "I'm Dalton."

She stops her nervous tic. "Rayna," she whispers as if I asked. Or as if I care.

"Cool." It's not cool, but whatever. "It's called Somerset House?" I verify, because what else would one talk about with a perfect stranger? Sports? World events? I'd rather die.

"Yeah, right off exit twelve."

We drive in silence. The smell of her blood hangs over me. "What happened to you, anyway?" I finally ask, because why the hell not?

She drops her gaze to the door handle, and her hand reaches for the metal. "I got jumped."

"Seems like it was more than that."

Her gray eyes leap toward me. "What makes you think that?"

Using my chin, I gesture toward her crotch. A blood stain that looks pretty unrelated to the rest of her injuries marks the fabric. Maybe she has the unfortunate luck of getting jumped *and* getting her period the same night. Or something worse happened to her. Something where someone would do all that to her head to silence her for good.

Her nostrils flare. "It's nothing."

"Nothing doesn't bleed." That is a fact.

She shrugs. "Fair. It's nothing I want to talk about, though."

I wouldn't want to talk about why I was found bloody and broken on the side of the road either. So I let it go.

She keeps looking at the time on my dashboard. Her knee shakes, bouncing up and down in the most irritating way.

A big house comes into view around a blind corner, and a sign with white letters welcomes us to Somerset House. I still can't tell what this place is. It sounds like the name of a bed-and-breakfast, but it sure doesn't look like one. It looks clinical. Like an office building or something.

I pull into the parking lot, and her eyes remain on the clock as it reads 9:20 p.m. I consider inviting her to my house instead of this hotel—or whatever the fuck it is—but I also have sub-zero interest in bringing anyone into my apartment. So this is where she will stay.

She lowers the visor and opens the cover to the mirror. Lights flash on and she rubs at the blood on her temple. She gets most of it off her pale skin, then covers the injury with her nearly black hair. She unclips her seatbelt, and I reach out for her before she can exit the car.

It's a stupid move, but I couldn't let her leave without tasting her. Her scent has been titillating me for the last fifteen minutes. She exhales as I lick my finger and rub it along a streak of leftover blood on her cheek.

"There you go," I tell her. "You look as good as . . . Well, you look okay."

This is when a look of fear, disgust, or anger should replace the look on her face because I just smeared her blood on my fingers. But her eyebrows don't furrow. Her lips don't draw into a deep frown. She displays none of the usual reactions, and it's fucking weird. Not even my own mother could control her discontent around me. This is so odd. Different.

And I think I like the difference.

She's awkward. She's . . .

Fucking magnificent.

She draws her face away and opens the car door. "Thanks," she whispers before getting out.

I nod at her and watch as she heads through the main door. A curfew sign hangs beside it, its janky hands marking 9:30. She just made it with minutes to spare. But what hotel has curfews?

Whatever, not my problem anymore. *She's* not my problem.

I draw my finger toward my lips. My tongue eases out of my mouth and swipes the calloused pad of my finger so I can taste her sinfully delicious blood. It's like nothing I've ever tasted. The moment the metallic bite finds my tongue, it seals itself inside my memory. With her life force inside me, she begins to occupy all my thoughts. I forget how tired I was. How draining today has been. I just think about Rayna, with her secretive story and tasty blood. I imagine tonguing every inch of blood from her body, ending with the source between her legs. I'll lap up the remnants of whatever harm came to her this evening, healing her with my unconventional tongue. One that craves blood.

Hers.

Chapter Three

Rayna

I rush inside, and the big clock above the front desk illuminates my near failure. Each ominous tick reminds me of what's at stake. As I close the door behind me, the big hand reaches thirty minutes on the hour. Saved with seconds to spare.

Lucy—our evening-shift house mom—gives me a disapproving look before turning her attention back to her phone. She gestures to the clipboard in front of me, and I sign back in to sober living in the knick of time.

She doesn't ask questions, which is odd. If I saw me, I'd have a lot of questions. I dig through my backpack and pull out the brass room key. I rub the warm metal between my fingers. We only lock our doors if we leave our personal space. Probably in case we overdose in our rooms one day.

The moment I step inside my room, into the comfort of my current "home," the crushing weight of what happened this evening bears down on me. I shiver when I recall my assault, but my trembling is eased by thoughts of the man who picked me up after such a god-awful night. His dark, nearly black hair was a mess on his head, and his ice-gray eyes kind of made him look blind. He clearly wasn't, because he was driving. He just looked haunted. Seems it too. Not sure what the hell happened to him in his life, but he was a strange dude.

I touch the place on my cheek where he swiped his finger along my skin to get rid of a trace of my blood. Who does that to a stranger? Yes, definitely a strange dude. But I couldn't ignore the fact that he didn't try to touch me beyond that. His hands didn't wander lower. I didn't have to fight him off. The distance he created between us pulled me closer. It attracted me. The space was a safety I haven't known in a long time.

I grab my bag and head down the hall to the large shared bathroom. I slip into the women's side and pray no one else is inside to see my injuries. I'm not in the mood to answer any questions or hide from a nosy gaze.

I walk into the bathroom and flip on the light. The fluorescent bulbs hum within their cracked plastic fixtures. I look in one of the mirrors to assess just how much damage my body has taken this time. My hand brushes through my long, dark hair. I didn't just get high earlier; I went and bought midlife-crisis blonde hair bleach too. I hope his wife finds it somewhere in the back of his shitty car. Blood and dirt cling to my hair, leaving it a sticky mess. My fingers graze my face, and I flinch at the wound on my temple that came from that damn flashlight. The one that nearly knocked me out, but I pretended it did. He had sex with me one more time once he thought I was unconscious. I had no choice but to swallow my pain as he assaulted me.

I pull off my shirt with a pained groan. My rigid muscles tense further with every motion. When the bloodstained fabric falls, I rub my hand along more of my injuries. My de-skinned palms move along my abdomen and caress each bruise I sustained from the many punches to my gut. I remove my jeans and bend each knee. My skin tightens and strains with the simple motions, the flesh as torn as the denim. My panties are gone, and I can only assume they're somewhere in his car.

I should go to the police, but I can't. Even though I was the victim, I'll be seen as a perp to them in the end. Just another druggie whore who deserved everything she got.

My fingers graze my mound, touching dried blood from my assault. The tears finally fall at the touch of that sensitive skin. I'm not nearly as numb to assaults like this as I thought I was. Not at this moment, at least. By the time I scrub off this blood, I'll harden myself again, closing off to the ongoing trauma. It's the only mindset to have when I've chosen to bury myself too deep in this life.

I groan and turn on the shower. Water falls from the old showerhead, and I get inside, waiting for the water to warm up. The cold drops tighten my already taut skin, and I flinch. Finally, the spray warms and begins to soothe my troubled body. Red-tinged rivers swirl around the drain, and I lean against the tile wall until they run clear.

What am I even doing anymore?

It's not like I don't have options. I could beg my mother for forgiveness for the failure she thinks she raised. Then again, I'm still failing. I could go to the police and confess my sins and deal with the repercussions. Jail may suck, but it might be better than relapsing more than today. But I'm a stubborn bitch, and I really wouldn't look good in a jumpsuit again.

I don't have much time left in Somerset House. I should

just stick it out and get this over with. Trying a little harder to stay clean would probably help as well.

I finish cleaning up, then I let the hot water soothe my aching bones for a few more minutes before getting out. I always feel reborn after a shower like that. As if the water can lick away my wounds and leave me unmarked. It can't, but for a moment, I feel whole.

The thick cotton towel scratches my body as I wrap it around myself. I flick off the bathroom light, and the hum gives way to silence. With wet, bare feet, I head back to my room. The moment I'm inside, I'm drawn to lights reflecting off the window, and I make my way to it so I can close the curtain. I peer past the finger smudges and see the man in the SUV still idling in the spot he pulled into to drop me off. I can't see what he's doing, but why is he still here? It's creepy. He probably can't see me, but I don't risk it. I pull the curtain closed, then ease it back just enough to watch him. My fingers clutch the towel against me as a sudden unease creeps over me. The man who made me feel kinda safe not that long ago is now seriously weirding me out.

Why are men so fucked up? And why am I still watching his damn car?

Dalton

WITH THE TASTE of her blood in my mouth, I couldn't drive home. Not yet. Her life force swirls around inside my mind and makes me horny as fuck. Can't say blood has ever made my dick this hard before. An unbearable throb sends an ache through my lower gut.

Don't Stop

I unzip my pants and pull out my cock. I rub myself in long strokes as I suck my lower lip into my mouth and taste the little bit of her that remains. She's all but gone from my skin, yet I can taste her as if she's bleeding directly into my mouth. It's that strong. That intense.

I drop back my head and focus on the tip of my dick as I imagine my tongue on her body. In this vision, I'm cleaning her of all remnants of pain. Fuck. I want to devour all of her until her blood becomes one with mine. Until I drink most of her.

She's still perched at her window, staring directly at my car. She doesn't realize I can see her silhouette behind the curtain. She shouldn't be able to see what I'm doing, though. She doesn't know I'm stroking myself to her. The curtain slides back, revealing more of her to me. I stare at the white towel wrapped around her. The soft peaks of her breasts swell above the folded fabric.

I bring my finger to my lips and suck away the last bit of her that clings to my skin. The sweet metallic taste tightens my balls. My abdomen curls as I chase my selfish pleasure. Come spills down my hand as my strokes grow ragged. I wipe it off with the bloodied napkin from the bird incident and take a deep breath as I tuck myself away.

Rayna slams her tightly clenched knuckles on the thick-paned windows, and I meet her angry, accusatory glare. I panic at the thought of her seeing what I've just done. She couldn't have, could she? The narrow, pissed-off glare sure looks like she might have. The curtains rip across the rod, but she continues peeking from the corner.

I gotta go before she thinks I'm too creepy. I mean, I *am* being creepy, but I don't want her to think so. I can't say I've ever felt such an intense desire to spill my load at the thought of some girl. I never think about women like that.

Usually I'm too annoyed by their very presence to imagine sleeping with them. But Rayna didn't annoy me. She's the first person I've wanted to spend more time with. Just a little longer.

But that was it. This is the last time I'll see her. I jerked off to an attractive stranger, and now I have to go back to my quiet apartment and try to remember that I hate everyone, including the strange girl I picked up on the side of the road.

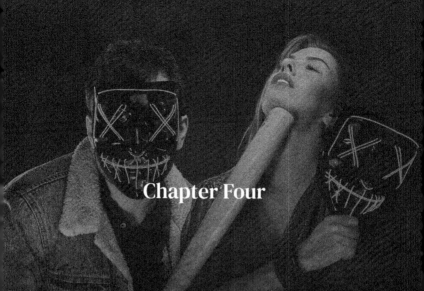

Chapter Four

Rayna

Independence is a beautiful thing, but it's a lonely existence too. For me, being independent means keeping myself out of jail and staying sober, and I'm fucking up royally at that last part. They even told me to keep away from cigarettes. Do they want to kill me? Do they want me to kill myself?

I pass the desk as I go outside to do exactly what they told me not to, which is smoke a fucking cigarette. They can get over it. At least it's not meth. Lucy jabbers on the phone as I pass the front desk, discussing the shit paint job in this place. The outside is quite nice and welcoming, but it's a dump on the inside. They hide the dark souls behind a pretty exterior for the public, but they didn't seem to care as much about how the dark souls feel once they're inside. I guess they're starting to care a little more now, which is nice.

She's still arguing about prices as I pass. Perfect. I can

sneak by without having to explain myself. I need a smoke before I go insane.

When I get outside, I go to the side of the building—it's painted a nice, casual tan—and slide down the wall. I light my cigarette, bring it to my lips, and watch people coming and going from the building. Sometimes it's one of us, in various states of shock and lostness. Other times it's the men and women in suits who monitor us.

The shocked and the lost.

I appreciate places like Somerset House as an option outside of jail, but there's no connection to other humans here, even though we're surrounded by them. We're told we can't fraternize with others who struggle with the same problems, yet that's all this house contains. I mean, the advice makes sense. If we hung out, we'd probably sit and talk about how badly we could use a fucking hit of literally anything, or how much better this place would be if we were high.

I would. So I stay by myself.

But that doesn't solve the problem of the incessant loneliness in a place like this. I'm sometimes torn between wanting to let someone into my life and furiously hating that idea. I don't attract the most savory people anyway, and I've never had a person in my life who hasn't hurt me in some form. People are shit. Hidden evils lurking beneath forced pleasantries. One man can so sweetly welcome me into his car and then assault me and decide he's going to kill me, then another will drive me home, completely uninterested in me. Then there's the mix—the guy who drives me home like a normie, then turns into a creep in the parking lot for a half hour after he dropped me off. People are weird and untrustworthy. Even knowing this, I can't help that inner draw to others of my species. My heart wants to connect with someone, but my brain very much says *the fuck you do.*

A minivan pulls into the parking lot. A dent caves in the right corner of the bumper, and the woman driving it looks exhausted. She parks and gets out before wrestling a baby from a car seat in the back.

Gross. I would rather suck on a meth pipe pulled directly from someone's dirty asshole than have a child.

The screeching cries from the infant gnaw at the nerves in my brain. It's unhealthy how disgusted I am by human offspring. The thought of having my own is even worse. I got an IUD the first chance I could because . . . no. Just not for me. I'm not sure how they're for anyone. I can't wrap my mind around it.

The woman carries the screaming little demon inside, and I wonder who she's visiting with that loud thing. No one I noticed looked like the "father" type. She should cut her losses and find someone else to provide genetic material for her hell spawn.

I inhale more smoke into my lungs as the sun's rays burn my pale skin. I touch my temple. The wound has scabbed over, and my jeans and long-sleeved black shirt cover the rest of my wounds. The dark clothing heats my skin until sweat drips down the curve of my back.

I make my way across the parking lot. I need a ride into the city. I need some new clothes. The shit I was wearing yesterday had to be tossed, and my fashion selection is limited as fuck at the moment. Asking the front desk for transportation makes me feel painfully inconvenient. It's easier for me to hitch a ride with someone. Well, when they don't end up doing what happened to me last night.

My eyes scan the parking lot for the least rapey person I can find. The man on a motorcycle is out because I'm pretty sure he lives here. Plus, motorcycles go right to my vagina, and fucking is probably considered fraternizing. Another man comes out after delivering something to the house. The brim of his hat hangs low over his eyes. He looks like a walking unnecessary risk. I don't see a lot of good options today.

The door slams and out comes the woman with her now-silent baby. She's cursing beneath her breath. Did the visit with her deadbeat baby daddy go poorly? Big surprise. I squelch my cigarette and stand up, brushing the dirt and rocks from the back of my pants before following her.

"Hey, can I get a ride?" I ask.

She turns to me with a frazzled haze to her tired eyes. Static runs through her blonde hair, as if she's been rubbing it in frustration. If she's visiting someone in there, it makes sense. We are frustrating.

"I don't have time," she says as she fumbles with the giant purse while trying to hold the little minefield in her arms.

"Here, give him to me," I say, and she hands him over with a noise that hints of equal parts annoyance and appreciation.

I hold the kid and wait for him to start crying as he reaches for strands of my hair. Some people would find this endearing, but I'm just frozen in place as I wait for this thing to detonate. His mom finds her keys buried in the great beyond of her purse, and she opens the back door. She takes the kid and puts him into his car seat, and beads of sweat gather on her brow as she fastens the buckles.

"Where do you need to go?" she asks, the annoyance still motivating every motion.

See, I can be fucking charming. I shrug. "Just somewhere to pick up some clothes."

"We're going to the mall," she says.

"That would be perfect."

She gestures toward the passenger seat and walks around the van. Bingo. And the best part is, she's a woman, and one who looks like she'd rather kill herself than me. So that's a win.

Dalton

I DIDN'T PUT two and two together until I pulled up to the same place I dropped off that girl yesterday. The tan building looks different in the daytime, and it doesn't appear as bad as they made it sound. I got the call this morning about the job, and the desperation in the woman's voice made it seem like I'd walk into something much worse than this.

Before I go inside, my eyes ride over to Rayna's window. The curtains are open and no one looks to be home, which is great. I don't really feel up to facing her questions about why I hovered outside for so long last night. While I could make up an excuse, I am shit at lying. She'd see straight through me. Avoiding her altogether is the better option.

As I push open a metal door and enter the building, a woman turns in her chair and greets me. "Hi, I'm Lucy. We spoke on the phone," she says, reaching toward me.

I don't make a move to grasp her outstretched hand, so she clears her throat and lowers her arm. I don't really touch people, which made it even weirder that I touched *her* last night. That girl. Rayna. The one who I sat up and thought about for an embarrassingly lengthy amount of time as I tried to sleep.

"Dalton," I say as my eyes scan the old building. It's not spectacular in here, but I've seen worse.

"Oh, I don't need the entryway painted. The owners made improvements to this area to make it more presentable to new clients, but we plan to change the paint scheme next year. We're focusing on the rooms right now."

"Alright," I say.

It's not presentable, but okay. Lines run through each stroke of paint, and I have to stop focusing on it before it makes me physically ill. It looks like they pulled an inflatable tube man from a car lot and handed him a paintbrush. Actually, that might have given them better results than this travesty. Maybe they can call me next year and I can fix this garbage paint job.

I stand by the front desk in a gross silence and wait for her to tell me where to go. Quiet like this is almost more stifling than actually being forced to engage. It's so painfully uncomfortable.

"Where am I working?" I finally ask before I reach my limit and just walk out and leave—which I've also done before.

Lucy stands up, locks her computer, and walks with me toward the back of the building. A long row of rooms with numbered doors line the wall in front of us. She knocks and opens the first door with a key. When we walk inside, my lips tighten. Disgusting walls crowd me on all sides. It's deplorable. This room alone will take longer than I'd hoped, but I can get started. I can't rush perfection.

The painting season always dies down near Halloween, which means these gigs might be the last before the season ends. Sure, I'll get on and off work for businesses and shit scattered through till things pick up again, but nothing as reliable as the spring and summer months. I should be thankful I have work at all this late in the year.

A grimace pulls my lips taut as I catch sight of peeling paint on every fucking wall. I'll have to sand first. Holes stare back at me, and my eyes hyperfocus on them. I can't stop staring at the jagged edges of drywall I'll need to patch.

Lucy follows my deadlocked gaze to an especially egregious hole. "Most of the people who come to sober living homes like this don't have the best coping mechanisms, so most of these rooms have holes of some kind. I'd rather them punch walls than each other, though," she says through a tight laugh.

Sober living home? Why did Rayna have me drop her off at one of these?

Realization smacks me like the naïve dumbass I am. If she lives here, she's probably struggling with addiction. Drugs and alcohol were never really my thing, but I can understand the allure. It'd be fun to escape my fucked-up little mind sometimes. Maybe I could chill and paint the walls a little less neurotically. But no, I always let my evil thoughts and feelings run rampant in my mind instead of silencing them. I think I'd miss their company if I quieted them now.

"I'll get my sh—stuff," I correct myself. Professionalism and shit.

I return to my vehicle and make two trips to bring in all the supplies I'll need. I'm not a contractor, but I can fix basic holes. I learned this particular skill when I put holes in my own walls and my mother would beat my ass and make me fix them.

"I think I'll fix all those holes before I even try to paint anything," I say to Lucy as I pass by the desk. "Can I have the master key so I can work on the other rooms when I finish this one?"

She digs in her pocket and slides the key into my palm. I nearly drop it when its body-heated warmth lands against my skin. Gross. I put it in my pocket and head down the hall.

I unlock the door and walk into the room she's already shown me. I get to work with joint compound and a putty knife on the first hole. Brisk fall air cools the world outside, yet it's hot as fuck in here. Sweat gathers beneath my clothes. I stop and look around, then take off my shirt and throw it over my shoulder as I keep working. I wouldn't be caught dead without my shirt if there were people around. So far, this place seems really fucking empty.

I swipe the sticky metal blade across the patch once more, my tongue clamped between my teeth as I try to perfect the lay of the plaster. Paint will cover it soon, but I want it to lie as flush as possible. I finish and wipe the blade on my pants, staring at my work with immense scrutiny. I'll probably need to sand the edges to get it just right.

When I look away from the wall, I see that girl staring at me from the hallway. A shopping bag hangs at her side, and her mouth gapes. She eyes me like I'm a finely carved statue in an art museum, and this is somehow worse than the usual looks of disgust or mortification I elicit from most people.

I back away, stumble on the corner of the bed, and fall back into the wall behind me. My elbow goes back, and I nearly create a new hole in the wall. I rip my shirt from my shoulder and throw it on. It sticks to my sweat-soaked body as I try to tug it down. How long was she watching me? *Why* was she watching me? It's fucking creepy.

Okay, I was creepy last night, but at least it wasn't face

to face. At least she didn't have to respond to me fucking her with my eyes.

Her lips draw up in a laugh, and I nearly trip again as I push away from the wall and yank at the hem of my shirt.

"What the *fuck*?" I snap.

"Don't like being watched?" she asks. Tou-fucking-ché.

I grab the putty knife from the floor and scoff. "I wasn't watching you."

"Sure," she says before she disappears down the hall.

I sneak toward the doorway and peer around the corner. She goes into the third door on the left. Two rooms down from this one.

"Bitch," I mutter under my breath as I gather my supplies and make my way to the room across the hall. How dare she judge me for doing the same thing she just did to me. I'm not doing her room unless I know she's gone.

She's strange. She's weird.

Like me.

Chapter Five

Rayna

Well, fuck. Imagine my surprise when I arrived at Somerset House and saw Sarah's door open. She wasn't in her room, but a shirtless dude was. And it was *the* dude from last night. The creep. But then I let myself be creepy because I couldn't tear my eyes away from him. His jeans hung low on his hips, the tops of his boxer briefs peeking out. Muscles cascaded down his abdomen, and his arms rippled with every stroke of the blade in his hand. Sweat dripped down his body. *Dripped*. It was so fucking hot. His response to my staring was chef's kiss too. I've never seen a man get so fucking distraught from being looked at. I couldn't help but laugh because he was being a total hypocrite. I couldn't see through the dark tinted windows, but I know he was watching my window last night. As a woman, I can tell when someone is staring me down.

I pull the clothes from my bag and put them into my dresser. The creaky wood lets out a high-pitched groan as I close the drawer. My small taxidermy collection sits on top of the dresser, and I turn my attention to these creatures who offer me so much comfort. I stroke the fur of the little squirrel—the piece that started my collection. He has no ears. They've been lost to the years since its little heart last beat. I found him at an estate sale, and the owners practically gave him to me. He's really scary looking, but I love him.

A raccoon skull rests beside him, and I run my fingers over the tiny teeth. I'm so weirdly fascinated by death, and I love how my collection makes people uncomfortable when they walk into my room. At least I don't have to worry about someone stealing my shit. No one wants Van Gogh, my earless little squirrel, or Cardi, my stripper mouse on the miniature metal pole. I even have a pair of dog balls in a jar full of formaldehyde. A leather swath sits beside it, rolled up and tied, and various sized bones stick through the slits within. That's my collection of baculum—the penis bones of different mammals. How fun is that? I'd have a human baculum if humans weren't one of the rare mammals without a penis bone. It's called a *boner,* for fuck's sake.

When I first came to Somerset House, they tried to tell me I couldn't bring my collection with me. Thankfully—and unsurprisingly—no one removed anything from my backpack while I was awaiting release. No way would I leave any of this behind. They're all I have left from home, back when I had a real home. They'll have to get over their weird fear of these harmless dead things, especially since they deal with those of us who are almost dead ourselves by the time we wind up on their doorstep. Speaking of death, if someone doesn't taxidermy the fuck out of me when I die, I'll stay and haunt them for all of eternity.

Dalton

I TRY TO KEEP WORKING. I got one of three holes patched in the room across the hall from where she confronted me. It's not just the heat that's making me sweat, though. It's the accusation she's throwing around. True or not.

I set my putty knife on the weathered dresser and make my way across the hall toward her room. The knock echoes down the hall, and I half expect her to leave me standing out here. I'm not sure I would let me in either. No, I definitely wouldn't. But she does, and I push inside her room before anyone can come down the hall and see what's happening. I walk into her, and she takes a step back to match each step I take forward until I have her back against the wall. Does she feel the fiery heat of my eyes boring through her? I hope she does. Something draws my attention away from a hint of fear in her eyes—a weird earless squirrel on her dresser—but then my eyes rise back to her.

"You need to watch your mouth," I say. Despite the heat in my eyes, each syllable is ice cold.

She raises her chin. "About what?"

"The *incorrect* notion that I was watching you. You can't say shit like that. I'm trying to work here."

"You *were* watching me."

I hit the wall by her head and worry for a moment that I just created another hole I'll have to fix. My hand spreads and the disgusting mess of paint flakes beneath my palm. She's right. She's a hundred percent fucking right. I *was* watching her last night. But she doesn't need to blast it through my new place of employment. I can't risk losing this job when I have a long winter ahead of me. I need the pay to hold me over through the slow season.

"Regardless of what I was or *wasn't* doing last night, you need to keep your mouth shut about it. You got to creep on me shirtless. At least you had a towel on!"

A smirk raises her lips. "See, you were watching me."

Fucking A. Goddamn it. "Fine, Rayna. I watched you for a little while. But that's it. Let it go. Pretend it didn't happen."

She bites into her lower lip as her haunting eyes rove down my chest. "I saw you looking at my collection."

"Wh-What?" I stammer.

She gestures behind me with her chin. "My death collection."

"Okay?" I say. Where the fuck is she going with this?

Her eyes sparkle, I swear. "You didn't look twice at it. You didn't think it was weird?"

I look back at her trove of undead treasures. It *is* weird. It's a weird fucking thing to have. But I don't see weird things as something to be grossed out by or uncomfortable around. I'm weird, and I like weird things. Like blood, whether it's from the living or dead or dying. I'm not the person to judge oddities when I am the farthest thing from normal myself.

I force my gaze back to her because this isn't the time for her to cream herself over the fact that her level of strange doesn't bother me. Nothing bothers me except other humans and lines in the fucking paint.

"Can you focus?" I say. "Will you please shut the fuck up about me watching you? I stared at you, then you stared at me. Let's call it even." I dig my nails into the wall beside her head. Paint flakes off and floats down to the old hardwoods. I hate that looking right into her eyes doesn't make me want to avert my own. I don't feel the usual panic choking my throat when talking to people.

"Fine!" she clips. "Get out of my room." The moment of weird flirtation washes off her face, just like that.

I drop my hand and turn to leave, but I stop at her collection. I touch the coarse hair of the weird, earless squirrel.

She hurries over and pushes my hand away. "Don't touch Van Gogh!"

"Where are his ears?"

Her lips tighten into a thin, angry line. "They fell off. He's, like, forty years dead."

When I drop my hand to my side and don't even blink at her response, I see the corners of her lips rising again. She's making this fucking weird. She's got a dresser covered in dead shit, but that isn't what's weirding me out. It's the flirty sparkle in her eye.

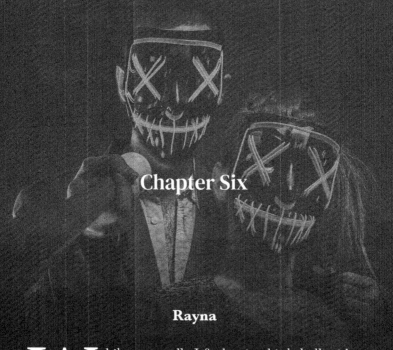

Chapter Six

Rayna

While on a walk, I find a tiny bird skull with a piece of foliage stuck through one of the nasal cavities. The bones feel so fragile. So light. And the spindly brown twig sticking through it looks like it might break off one of the bones. Despite that, it's really pretty. Nature has plucked it clean of all flesh, and it did a better job than some of the pieces I've done myself. I'm bringing it home with me. I have the perfect place for it on my dresser.

Every time a car drives by, I throw my thumb into the wind, but no one stops. I shift my bag to the other side and hold it up again, but I'm forced to make the entire trek on foot. By the time I get back to Somerset, I'm tired and craving a hit of anything. I haven't gotten high since the night it put me in the car with the suburban dad from hell. Thankfully, enough time has passed and it didn't show up on my random urine test this morning. I nearly chewed off the tips of my fingers with nerves while waiting for that result. That was one of the worst nights of my life, and the high hadn't been worth it. If that momentary relapse had sent me back to jail, it would have added insult to injury.

I walk down the hall, my hair sticking to my cheeks. Even though it's cooler out, the walk home has soaked me with sweat. Most of the doors are closed like normal, and I wonder how far Dalton has gotten with his hole fixing and painting. I saw Sarah's room yesterday, fully painted, and it looked fucking nice. It felt more like a home instead of somewhere they shoved us as an afterthought. Which is what they did.

I stop outside my door. It's unlocked and cracked open. This dude better not be in my room without me. I don't like anyone in there because of my collection. I don't worry about people stealing it, but I worry about people fucking with it and damaging any of my treasures. Some are fragile as fuck. Like Van Gogh. Many of the pieces have been dead longer than these people have been alive.

I push open the door, and he looks as surprised as me. He's on a ladder, his tall body reaching upward as he paints the delicate corner where the ceiling meets the wall. When he sees me, he stumbles back and spreads gray paint on the ceiling, then curses and catches himself before he falls.

"I thought you were gone," he says. His chest heaves as he eyes the gray paint marring the white ceiling he'd already finished. "Fuck," he whispers.

"Yeah, I came back. If I knew you were doing my room today, I wouldn't have left."

"Are you worried I'll steal your ghoulish little collection?" he asks with an annoyed snip. He wipes his hand onto his pants, leaving a smear of gray behind.

I scoff and pluck the fragile bird skull from my bag and

set it on top of a dark perfume bottle lid. A skull wraps around the bottle, the label another display of glorious death. I don't wear it—the scent is too flowery and strong—but the bottle was too pretty to pass up. The little branch with a single leaf still sticks from the skull's nasal cavity. The branch and leaf will finish dying and will match the skull soon enough, so I leave it in place.

I drop my bag to the floor, letting it hit with a heavy thud that makes him jump. I sit on my bed, staring at the weird fucking dude having a panic attack over a little paint snafu. He keeps dabbing that brush, over and over, but he's not doing anything with it.

"Can you leave?" he asks.

"No, it's my room."

He sets the brush on the ladder. "I don't work around people. I can't."

"Why? You don't want people to see you having a nervous breakdown over some paint on the ceiling?"

"Fuck you," he says, and it makes me smile.

But I don't leave. I just scoot backward on the bed and rest my back on one of the unpainted walls. "So professional."

He stomps down the ladder, walks over to me, and lifts a paint-covered hand to my throat, pinning me against the wall. "You *don't* want to fuck with me, bones."

My immediate reaction to him putting his hand on me is to bring up my knee and plant it right in his gut. He releases me with a grunt, then his hands grip the footboard as he draws in his abdomen to take a heavy, angry breath. His haunting eyes look like they want to kill me in seven different ways and pose me on my dresser with the rest of my creepy things.

"No, fuck *you*, creep," I say.

I stand up and walk toward the ladder. I climb the treads and grab the paintbrush covered in nice gray paint. His eyes widen and he opens his mouth to yell at me, but I brush the paint above my head and ruin more of his perfect white ceiling before he can utter a word.

Dalton

SHE DIDN'T. She did *not* just fucking do that. The half-assed line of gray paint brushing over the ceiling I perfected before she came barging in makes me see red. More specifically, I envision sawing at her throat with the fucking putty knife until the hand clutching my brush grows limp and motionless.

It's been a while since I've had such homicidal thoughts, but they've risen to the forefront of my mind more often lately. I almost thought I outgrew them. They'd grown so distant, I even wondered if they had all been a delusion to begin with.

But here I am, committing a violent homicide in my mind all over again.

I rush the ladder and we fight for control. She tries to kick at me, and I try to claw her down. Strangled sounds come from her throat as we fight. I finally grip her arm and bring her to the bottom step. Her legs slide between mine as her ass hits the step above it. The moment she's there, a fierce look overtakes her face and I know she plans to go for my nuts. I pin her with my body and my crotch so she can't lift her legs. With her hand still wrapped around the handle of the paintbrush, she swings her arm. A swatch of gray lands on my shirt before she drags the brush right across my fucking face. As the cold, sticky paint clings to my skin, I grab her wrist and pin it behind her. This rocks the ladder and sends the paint can onto its side, spilling a waterfall of gray over the side and onto the floor.

She has no fucking idea what a mess she's made. Even so, the thought of leaning in and kissing her is a pleasurable one for me. A longing I can hardly stand experiencing in the first place.

I fist her hair and she whimpers. "Why'd you do that?"

"Because you're being a jerk, and it's unhealthy to be that obsessed over fucking paint."

My eyes narrow. "I just take pride in my work.".

"It's more than that. You've killed me three different ways in the last five minutes, haven't you?" Her eyes harden on me. "Haven't you?"

How'd she know? Can she see my homicidal tendencies on my face? In my expression? In my heart?

My lips tighten, but I release her and walk to her dresser. Her eyes widen as I grip her weird little squirrel, smearing a bit of paint on its off-white chest. I hold it out in front of me. "It's not healthy to be this obsessed with dead things, either."

Her eyes go from wide to narrow as she looks at me the same way I looked at her when she dragged paint across the ceiling. She's probably killing me in her mind as we speak. And that's how she knew.

Like recognizes like.

She rushes over to me, and I hold the squirrel above my head. Her cheek presses against my stomach as she tries to claw and reach her macabre little toy; she's too fucking short to grasp it.

"If you break Van Gogh, I will break you!" she squeals.

An angry, feral growl runs through her words. So cute. "Give him back!"

The desperate anger on her face forces me to consider it, but I disregard her emotions as my eyes land on the gray abomination running across the corner of the ceiling. I turn my attention back to the scrappy woman fighting to reach the squirrel in my raised hand. "Have you killed me yet, bones? Murdered me in your mind?"

Her chest careers into me as she tries to climb my torso to lay her hands on her prized possession. "I'm about to murder you in real life!" Something tells me she would. If a knife was right here, she'd use it on me. She's got that unhinged glare that I recognize in my own reflection sometimes.

"I'm taking this with me," I say, and my words make her drop both her feet to the ground as her eyes bore into me. "When I come to fix that ceiling tomorrow, I'll give back your stupid squirrel."

Her eyes dart as she looks between me and the squirrel. "If anything happens to Van Gogh, I will fucking remove every single part of you that's missing on him."

The ferocity in her tone goes straight to my dick. An undeniable certainty punctuates each word. If Van Gogh's little balls fall off—if he even still has them—mine will be next. I don't plan to tear apart her hideous emotional support taxidermy, though. It's a security deposit that ensures I'll see her again. Oddly enough, that's what I want more than anything.

I take the squirrel to my car and lock it in my trunk, then I return to her room to gather my things and wipe up the spilled paint before it sets. She sits on her bed, pouting as she watches me with a hate-filled glare.

Don't Stop

Before exiting her room, I turn to face her a final time. "See you tomorrow, bones."

Chapter Seven

Rayna

I stare at the vacant space on my dresser where Van Gogh used to be. White-hot anger fills me. I bite my nails as I worry if he's okay. If he's being taken care of. If that fuck is putting him in direct sun, which could damage his fur. My eyes move to the dried gray paint on the ceiling. *That* didn't warrant him taking something that belonged to me. It's fucking stupid. I bet he cries if he spills a glass of milk too.

I get out of bed, walk down the hall, and stop at the desk.

"How can I help you, Rayna?" Lucy asks.

"Do you have a Sharpie I can borrow?"

She digs around in a desk drawer until her fingers find a thick black marker. It's magnificent. She hands it to me. As I walk back to my room, a glorious excitement fills me. He's coming to fix the ceiling, but he'll have a fucking coronary when he sees what I have in store.

I wrap my fingers around the marker's top, pulling until

it twists off with a creak. I lean against the wall and bring the marker to my nose with a deep sniff. The chemical smell singes my sinuses, and I remember when people used to claim these things could get you high. They can't, not really, but the smell reminds me of times I tried. I turned to more concrete methods after that, but huffing fumes didn't turn into my "thing." It just rendered me unconscious after giving me a floaty feeling for three measly seconds. Total waste of money, especially when I discovered things that could get me high for hours—or days—on end.

Now I'm riding another high. The anxiety has built to a crescendo in my brain, and if I don't do something to pop the pressure valve, I'll explode.

So I start writing.

I drag the marker over the gray wall, spilling my rage in big, blocky letters. *Creep. Freak. Weirdo. It's only paint.* I add a colorful swatch of swear words, then sign it off with my new nickname.

Bones.

When the high of my anger wears off and I look at the mess I made, I feel bad for what I've done. I struggle with anger issues and impulse control, and while I can usually control myself—or smother my urges with drugs—I didn't this time. What I did is nothing major. Kids do this shit all the time. But this will likely send Dalton into a category-five-hurricane-level panic. It's going to be like finding out the apocalypse is unfolding right in front of his pale eyes the moment he walks in here and sees my handiwork all over his precious paint.

I need to fix this.

I grab a bottle of hand sanitizer, put it on the wall, and try to rub it out with my shirt. It smears and spreads the ink, making it worse, and the ghost of each letter remains within the smudges. While I'm furiously circling the ominous black ink, the door to my room opens. I hate that they gave him a master key. He shouldn't be allowed to just barge in here and see what I did!

And boy, does he.

His lower jaw drops as he takes in the smudges and scribbles, and I swear those gray eyes take on a red cast as he scans everything I've done.

"What. The. Fuck!" he yells. His voice has risen to a level that endangers both of us by putting us at risk of getting in trouble.

"Someone broke in! See? I'm trying to clean it off." I showcase my half-assed cleanup job, then go back to scrubbing the wall. "Fucking kids."

With his lips formed in a tight, angry line, he walks closer to the wall adjacent to me. "You're trying to tell me that some stranger came in here, wrote some really relevant statements, and signed my nickname for you at the bottom? The nickname I gave you only yesterday?"

I drop my gaze. I'd forgotten that I'd signed it in bitchy, bold letters. I even underlined it.

He throws down his supplies and his backpack and turns around and leaves. I dig through the black paint-stained bag the moment he exits the room. My hands fumble past his phone, a sweater, and a laptop, but I see no sign of my beloved Van Gogh. Fucking liar. Moments later, he returns with a gray paint can.

My balled fists land on my hips. "Where's Van Gogh?"

He grabs the ladder from against the wall and sets it up. Gray paint still stains the metal. He places his roller brush, pan, and a white can of paint on a shelf, then he begins climbing the ladder. He does all of this without answering my question or even acknowledging that I've spoken.

"I said, where's my fucking squirrel?" I repeat.

He doesn't look back at me as he starts painting the ceiling in smooth, dedicated strokes despite the anger I see racking his body. "It's at home. I forgot it, and you should be fucking grateful. If I saw this and I had your precious little squirrel in my possession, I'd have ripped his fucking head off." The strokes of his brush never change speed or pressure, just like his voice, and he delivers the last sentence with an eerie calmness that sends a nail through my gut.

"If you rip his head off, yours is next. Fucking dick!" I scream.

He finishes obliterating the gray streak on the ceiling, then he sets the brush on the top of the ladder. "He's dead already, Rayna." He climbs down, each step making a hollow noise beneath his feet. "But I *will* set him on fucking fire when I get home if you don't paint these two walls you fucked up."

He grabs my arm, pulls me toward the wall, and shoves a brush handle into my hand. I scoff, press the roller to the wall, and push it in sloppy strokes because I know it will annoy him. A frustrated growl comes from deep inside him, and he wraps his hand around mine. The way his angry breath beats on my neck as he raises my hand to the wall makes my chest hitch. The grip on my hand is harsh, but he rolls the paint over the wall in a gentle motion. Each pass creates a smooth finish. Linear as fuck.

The warmth of his body burns me as he stands right behind me and forces me to paint what I fucked up in the first place. Painting like this, lining up each stroke with the last, is oddly relaxing. A less frustrated groan leaves his lips. It's still frustrated, but in a different kind of way. The sound buries itself in my pelvis. This dude must really like painting. Intimately. Like, he has a fetish for it or something.

Then his cock hardens behind my back, confirming my suspicions.

Fucking. Weirdo.

At the last stroke, he turns me around and fists my hair. My heart thumps against my chest as he dips his finger into the paint and pushes it into my mouth. It shocks me so much that I drop the roller from my hand. The bitter, mouth-drying taste assaults my tongue. The paint dries every mucous membrane I have, and I feel like I've sucked on a disgusting gray lemon. My lips pucker around his finger.

"I hope it tastes awful, bones," he says. A spark lights his eyes, and I can't begin to understand its meaning. "If you fuck with my shit again, you'll suck your blood off my fingers instead of this paint."

Chapter Eight

Dalton

My car sputters, and I wonder if we've finally reached the end of our road together. "Not today, buddy." I rub the steering wheel to encourage the poor thing to keep going. Finally, it roars to life and I head to the Somerset with a copy of the master key burning a hole in my pocket.

I shouldn't have made a copy, but I did. I can't help myself. Even after she destroyed my hard work, I'm drawn to her. Besides, I told her I'd drop off her squirrel.

I just didn't say when.

I drive to Somerset House and pull into the dark parking lot. No lights shine within the building's interior because it's almost midnight. I creep toward the main door and close my hand around the handle. It's locked, and my master key only works on the interior doors. I didn't consider this complication. I walk over to her window and pray it's open. When it gives, slipping open and letting warm air suck in the outdoor breeze, a smile slides onto my face. I lift it the rest of the way, place my bag on the ground, and climb inside before anyone notices me.

I drop my feet to the floor and gather my bearings for a moment before realizing I can't reach my bag on the ground outside. Rather than climbing out and in again, I leave it. I'll have to return her squirrel another day.

I turn toward the bed. She's sleeping, her lips soft and loose. For a second, I imagine kissing them, then my thoughts turn to biting them off and how much they'd bleed. Tasting her, fresh from the source . . .

I need to think about something else.

A pill bottle on her nightstand catches my attention, and I pick it up, careful not to shake up the pills inside. Turning the label to face me, I realize they're heavy-duty sleeping pills. The label also reveals that these pills aren't prescribed to her. My doctor put me on this same medication before. They would put me to sleep, sure, but then they went a step beyond sleep and made me black out. I would wake up and interact with people—as I was told on several occasions—but I remembered none of it when I woke up.

I place the bottle back in its spot and turn back to Rayna. Her cami twists around her torso and her tits nearly slip from beneath the thin fabric. Unable to stop myself, I reach toward her and stroke the soft inside of her arm. Her skin is like suede beneath my fingertips. My cock hardens and I rub a hand down the front of my pants. It's been a long time since I've wanted to have sex with anyone but myself. The fear of disappointing a partner is enough to make anyone become abstinent, so I usually avoid it. She doesn't look at me with that same disgust that others do, though, and that makes me rock hard.

When she doesn't stir from my touch on her inner arm, I move my hand to her chest. Even as I slip the fabric away and expose the soft, pink nipple that pressed against it, she remains asleep. My fingers dig into the flesh of her breast, and I ache for her. Her level of unconsciousness adds another layer to the growing desire running through my body. If she stays asleep, there's no way I can disappoint her.

Yes, I want to fuck her.

I lower the sheet and rub my hand between her legs until my fingers reach her tiny black shorts. The fabric slips aside and gives me a view of the prettiest pussy I've ever seen. A faded bruise paints her inner thigh, and I wonder if it's from the night I first met her. Remembering how she looked that first night sends a tightening coil through my gut as I put my finger and thumb on her lips and spread them. I wish blood still marked her skin so I could lick her clean.

I lean down and inhale her scent—sweet, like cherries and almonds, with a hint of sweat and soap. I bring my nose closer to her neatly shaved mound, inhaling even more of her. A heady musk clings to the fine brown hairs. It's not an unpleasant smell. It's a scent that draws me closer to her. It calls to me and demands I put my tongue on her.

So I do.

I slip my tongue between my lips and swipe from her hole to her mound, taking every bit of her into my mouth. She tastes fucking incredible. She'd taste better covered in blood, but this is almost as good. The moment my tongue touched her, I wanted more of her. I want my tongue on every fucking inch of her body. I lift her shirt and lick from her hole to her mound again, then I travel to her navel. It's not enough. I need more. I move toward her breast, taking the hardening nipple into my mouth and sucking the sweat from her skin. I lick upward, moving to the curve of her clavicle and continuing to her throat. I hover there. I want to swipe my tongue across her lips, but something holds me back. Probably the fear that I won't be able to stop myself from biting them until they bleed once that supple skin touches my tongue.

I work open my jeans as I lick and suck the curve of her neck. My shoes slide away from my feet, and I climb into bed with her. Her thighs are so fucking soft as I hook them over mine and pull her into me. She stirs a bit as her head shifts positions, but her eyes remain closed.

I lean over her. "Shh, go back to sleep," I whisper. "I *need* to fuck you."

Her jaw loosens again, but she doesn't respond. I grip the head of my cock and push inside her, slow and easy. I need to feel her pussy take each inch of my cock. It's incredible. I grip the sheet beside her head as she slowly devours my dick. A groan leaves my lips when I can go no further. She's taken all of me.

"Good girl, bones," I growl as my lips fall back to her neck. But I can't stick to her neck. I give in and capture her mouth, kissing lips I imagined doing so much more with. They're as plump and soft as I expected, and I find myself biting into her lower lip. She whimpers as I taste the fresh metallic tang of her blood. Her eyes flutter open, and I release her lip from my teeth.

"Am I dreaming?" she asks, a confused haze in her voice that makes me certain she's in that weird awakened state I experienced while on those drugs. Her chest lifts into me as she scrambles to her elbows with disconnected movements.

"Yes, it's just a sexy fucking dream. Now lie down and go back to sleep. Just let me fuck your little cunt."

I put a hand to her throat and ease her onto her back. She's too out of her mind to fight me, so she lies back and closes her eyes. A soft moan leaves her lips. She truly believes this is a dream, and her lack of disgust excites me. She just relaxed and moaned for me.

I sit up and tug her thighs against me again to adjust her and pull her deeper into me. My eyes focus on each motion I make, pulling out of her and pushing back inside. Slow and methodical. My length appears and disappears inside her again. It's an intoxicating sight. Her sexy little pussy stretches around my cock, and I moan and dig my fingers into her thighs. She feels so fucking good. I can't imagine how she'd feel if she were awake and fucking me back. Moving her hips and taking all of me. Every single inch.

"Dalton," she whispers, her voice heavy with sleep.

"Yes, bones?" I lean over her, bringing my mouth close to hers but not grabbing her perfect lips again.

"Did you bring back my squirrel?"

A smile tugs at my lips. "Not tonight. Tonight, I brought you something else I wanted to give you."

"What is it?" she whispers, eyes still closed.

"I want to give you all my come. I want to empty my balls inside you, then lick you clean."

"Okay." Her voice fades at the end, as if she's falling asleep once more, but now I kind of want her awake. I want her lost in this "dream" she thinks she's in.

"Stay awake for me," I tell her, giving her a smack on her cheek.

"I can't," she whines. "I'm tired."

Instead of being soft and careful with her, I increase the pressure and speed and drive her into the mattress. The headboard hits the freshly painted wall, but I can't stop. I lean down and bite her lip until I taste her blood again. It brings me to my edge. I moan, biting harder as I spill my come inside her. My hips stutter against her, and I pull out of her once my cock stops throbbing. I shouldn't have filled her, but I did. She felt too fucking good to pull out of. I threw all the risk aside to fill her.

White beads of come drip from her. I lie between her legs and catch it with my tongue, driving it upward and stuffing it inside her. I tongue-fuck her, tasting her sweetness as it combines with my salty come. I place my lips around her entrance and suck until I draw every drop into my mouth. I'll leave no trace of what happened tonight. She can think it was just a *really* good dream.

Once I've cleaned her, I drag my tongue upward and eat her pussy. Devour her. Flick her clit. When she doesn't wake up, I sink my teeth into the most sensitive part of her body until she finally bucks her hips into my face. Her hands hit me, and I release my grip and return to lashing her clit with my tongue. She moans, low and soft, and her hands go from hitting me to pulling my shirt into her pleasure-clenched fists.

I rake my teeth over her hood before going back to licking her, and each motion of my tongue makes her curl her hips against my mouth.

"Are you going to come, bones?" I growl against her slit, which spreads before me from the excitement of her clit. "I want you to grind into me and soak my fucking face."

Her thighs tremble and she rocks her hips with slow, disconnected movements that pull my face deeper until she soaks my chin with her come. She's a dripping, wet mess, and she doesn't even know I'm real. That *this* is real.

With her legs still trembling, I look at the window. I have to go.

"Lie with me, Dalton," she whispers, forcing my attention back to her.

I can't. Not after I fucking assaulted her, even if I made

her come. She's not in a position to consent to what I've done to her.

But something in the way she asks throws all caution out that window. I climb up beside her and lie down. I'll only stay until she falls asleep. When she wakes up tomorrow, she won't remember this. If snippets of what happened run through her mind, she'll tell herself it was all a wet dream.

She turns away and backs into me. I brush her hair away from her flushed cheek. A thin layer of sweat coats both of us. I wrap my arm around her, and a satiated moan leaves her lips.

"I'm sorry I ruined your wall," she says, just when I think she's asleep again.

"It's okay." It's not okay, but I say it anyway. It feels like the right thing to say with our come on my tongue and her wetness drying on my dick. "I'll bring your squirrel back tomorrow, okay?"

Maybe.

Chapter Nine

Rayna

I'm in a car with a guy. A stranger. As he drives toward Somerset House, I should focus on my safety and watch for any signs of danger, but my mind is stuck on last night. I dreamed about Dalton. That he came into my room, fucked me, ate me out, and even lay with me after. Dream me is delusional. Don't get me wrong, he's a good-looking guy, with soft, sweet features plastered on a really grumpy face. But he's a bit nuts. I am too, but still. He's not someone I would fuck.

Or is he?

I thought about it when he looked at my collection and didn't flinch. I imagined him pushing all my ghoulish shit aside and fucking me on that dresser. But then he acted like a dick, and I don't vibe with dicks.

We pull into the parking lot, and the driver steers the car toward a quiet corner before killing the ignition. I fidget as he takes his hand off the steering wheel and lowers the back of his seat, all the while staring at me with hard, hungry eyes. It's such a gross, desperate guy move. His hand reaches for mine, and I rip it away before he can place my palm on the swelling crotch of his jeans.

"I'm not doing that," I say. I swivel to get out of his car, but he reaches for me and rips me backward.

"I gave you a ride," he says.

God, I hate men. Almost every time I hitchhike, this is their idea of payment. Most people have an ulterior motive. Whatever happened to doing nice things because you want to do nice things?

He puts a hand around the back of my head and pushes my face onto his lap. He tries to hold on to me, but I flail and fight as he works open his jeans. Frustrated breaths fall from his heaving chest, and when he finally gets his jeans open, I'm faced with a harsh reality. I'm about to be assaulted again. With my head forced just inches from his lap and my strength waning, his door whips open and he releases me. I scramble backward and look into the face of a rage-filled silhouette standing just outside the open door.

Dalton.

He snatches the man into the evening twilight and starts beating the ever-loving shit out of him. It's beautiful. I climb out of the car to join the fray, and I send my knee into his nuts as Dalton pummels his face.

"What the fuck!" the man screams, spitting blood onto the ground. "She wanted it!"

Dalton turns toward me. "Sure didn't look like it. I've never had to physically pin someone to my lap for a consensual dick sucking." Rage burns through Dalton's eyes, and I fear he'll kill the guy if I don't intervene.

"Hey, let him go. He's just a creep," I tell him, before he takes things too far.

Dalton sucks in a deep breath and releases the man,

who then scrambles back into his car. Before he can close the door and drive away, Dalton rushes forward and grips his short hair, turning him to face me. "Apologize."

"What? No."

He draws back his arm again and the man flinches.

"I'm sorry! Okay? I'm sorry."

Dalton releases him and the man panics and nearly drives into the Somerset sign in his hurry to get the fuck out of the parking lot. I turn to Dalton. He holds his bloody hand against his abdomen.

"You okay?" I ask.

"Are you?"

I nod, then he does too. "You should come inside and clean that off."

He looks down at his hand and throws me another nod. We head inside, and he draws his sleeve over his hand to hide the blood as we walk past Lucy, who's too busy to notice us, anyway.

I bring him toward the shared-use bathroom, then I check to ensure it's empty. I'm not surprised when I find that it is. We've reached the part of the evening when people usually go out to eat or get high or drunk before curfew. The heavy door closes behind him once he joins me inside.

Before Dalton goes to the sink, he pulls back his sleeve and looks at the fresh blood soaking his skin. With a glassy look in his eyes, he lifts his fist to his mouth and laps the red areas with long, broad strokes of his tongue. Seeing it reminds me of my dream last night, and I imagine his tongue on me just like that. My reaction to that thought must have come across my face because he smirks at me.

"It doesn't bother you?" he asks as he raises his bloody fist and smiles. Red clings to his lips.

I shake my head. "Does it bother you that I like dead things?"

He shakes his head, and my heart flutters against my chest. This is a weird fucking conversation, and we are weird people. Why does that make me want to kiss him and taste the blood on his lips?

Dalton

I LOWER my tongue to my fist again, and she looks at me like she's fondly remembering her "dream." Remembering me. I see the glint of recognition all over her face as my tongue rides along my skin. She remembers what it felt like to have my tongue on her. There's no denying it.

She isn't the only one who's been thinking about it. Ever since yesterday, I've been unable to think of anything else. She's completely consumed me. I tried to paint and get on with work, but I couldn't keep my straight lines going. My mind was in too many places, mostly inside her. So I came back. I wanted to return her squirrel, that's all, but seeing someone trying to steal what has become mine—in my mind, at least—made me absolutely homicidal again. I imagined breaking his skull against his car before she told me to stop. Before she tethered me to reality once again.

She's steps into me now. She's so close. Her breath rolls against mine as she looks into my face with a perfect pout on her lips. She wants me to kiss her. I may be pretty bad with women, but I can tell that much. Now she's leaning in, closing the gap.

Fuck it.

I pull her into me and kiss her. Hard. Passionately. When I draw her lip into my mouth and bite down on that supple skin, she gasps at the pain. A look crosses her face, but I can't decipher its meaning. Anger and lust fight for dominance in her features, but neither can win when they're both overshadowed by intense confusion. I stand there with her mouth close to mine as she looks at me as if she either wants to lean in and kiss me again or pull back her fist and deck me between the eyes.

I need to come clean. She's confused because that bite on her lip reminds her of what I did last night. Of what I did in the vision she believes is a dream. This isn't fair to her. I put space between us before I confess, though, because I haven't forgotten what her knee can do.

"Are you remembering a dream last night?" I ask.

Her cheeks flush, and her eyes search mine. "How do you know?"

I take another step back before continuing. "Because it wasn't a dream."

Her mouth drops open. Her head shakes. Fear dances in her pale eyes before her expression flattens. "I don't believe you. I—"

I grab her arm and pull her to the mirror. I grip her lower lip and pull it down, forcing her to confront proof that last night wasn't a dream. My teeth marks stare back at her.

"You had sex with me while I was asleep?" she says.

I shrug. "When you were drugged. You were somewhat awake when you came on my face."

She turns to face me, then her hand draws back and collides with my cheek before I can move out of the way. The sound ricochets off the shower stalls and comes back to me. My cheek heats. Burns. I grab her and put her back against the smooth tile wall behind her, then I pin her arms above her head.

"Why?" she asks, a defiant growl in her tone.

"Because I *had* to have you, bones. I needed your body last night. I needed *you*."

Her lips tighten. "You can't just take things like that. I've had that happen to me too many fucking times for you to do it too."

With her hands still pinned by one of mine, I raise the other to her throat. She flails within my grasp, but I tighten my grip to keep her face still as I lean forward and kiss her. She takes my lower lip between her teeth and bites the shit out of it. Blood drips down my chin, but despite the intense pain, I can't stop exploring her mouth. The kiss intensifies, and her body begins to relax.

I release her hands completely and drop my guard as she pulls her mouth away from mine. If she plans to knee me in the nuts, now's the time, because I'm absolutely blind to anything around me aside from her. Instead, her finger moves to my chin and strokes my skin, gathering the blood. She brings it to her lips and puts it in her mouth, sucking on it.

That one action has placed me squarely in the palm of her hand. If she told me to kill myself right now, I would do it. I would bleed out for her so she can pose me like one of her grotesque little dolls in her room. I have never been so turned on.

"Fuck, bones," I growl. This can't be real life. She can't be real. Maybe *I'm* the one who's dreaming.

As her hand goes for my zipper and she drops to her knees, I'm positive I am. I told that dude I've never had to force a woman onto my lap for a blowjob, but truth be told, I've never had one at all. I've done everything else, but I've never felt anyone's warm mouth on me. I've never asked for it because it felt cringey and weird to do so, and my infrequent sexual partners from my past never offered.

But Rayna is offering now, and I'm too enthralled to tell her no. It's not until she has my dick in her hands that I worry she might bite me once her lips wrap around my cock. I draw my hips away from her touch, and her fingers graze my length.

"What's the matter? Afraid I'll hurt you?" she asks, biting into her lower lip. "What's the worst I can do? Make your cock bleed with my teeth? Don't act like you wouldn't love that in my mouth too."

Oh god, she's right. I would fuck her mouth and make her swallow every drop of my blood, closely followed by my come. The pain would be worth every second of the intense pleasure I imagine she'll bring me.

Again, fuck it.

I thrust my hips forward, filling her hand with my cock. She looks up at me with those hauntingly familiar eyes before opening her mouth and putting me between her lips. A low, gravelly moan escapes me as I lean forward to brace my hand against the wall. Her tongue swirls around the tip, heating my skin with every bob of her head. Fuck, she feels good. I knew she would, but I never imagined I'd get to experience her like this. So eager. So hungry for me.

I bury my free hand in her hair and fuck her mouth, and when I make her take me deeper, I fuck her throat. She gags and tightens her throat around my head.

"You're so good with your mouth. Why are you giving me this?" I ask. It's probably not the best time, but I want to know why she sank to her knees for me, especially after I told her what I did to her last night.

Instead of offering an answer, she sucks and strokes me until my balls tighten and my stomach clenches.

"I'm coming," I whisper. I think I'm supposed to ask her where she wants my come, but I'm too lost in the heat of the moment to form that question. I wrap my hand around my dick and pull back to stroke myself, keeping my head just behind her lips. My pleasure coats her tongue seconds later.

"Open your mouth," I tell her.

She rolls her eyes up to me and parts her puffy lips. Come gathers beneath her tongue, but it's not perfect. Not yet. I suck on the wound in my lip from when she bit me, and blood rises to the surface. Combining it with spit from my mouth, I lean over and drop the mixture onto her tongue. Red-streaked spit joins my come in her mouth, and now it's perfect.

"You didn't answer me," I say as I watch her tongue work around the mixture. "Why are you giving me your mouth after what I've done to you?"

She wipes the spit and blood from her chin before swallowing. "Because you didn't leave. You chose to lie with me after."

Chapter Ten

Rayna

He walks into my room and tries to avoid looking at my walls, as if he's afraid to see what I've done to them now. I haven't done anything. After he painted that section *with* me, I don't feel the need to fuck it up again.

He slips off his backpack and unzips it. Splotches of dried paint cover its ragged surface, just like his sweater. He pulls out Van Gogh and balances him on the palm of his hand. My eyes light up. I'm almost as excited as the day I first plucked him from a shelf at that estate sale. His fur looks a bit disheveled from being shoved inside his bag, and a smear of gray paint colors his off-white belly, but all of his fragile extremities remain attached. Thank god, because if something happened to Van Gogh, I'd have never forgiven myself for putting my mouth on the person who destroyed that squirrel.

I reach out for my precious pet, but Dalton lifts it above

his head again. I step into him, clawing at his body to get to Van Gogh. My nails dig into the insides of his arms.

"Give him to me, Dalton!" I say, raising my voice at his name. I jump, trying to climb him like a jungle gym to get my fucking squirrel.

"Not until you tell me what happened to you the night I picked you up." The soft and smooth way he speaks catches me off guard. Why does it matter to him? He assaulted me too. Not the same way, but just because he didn't make me bleed doesn't mean he didn't do something wrong. It's just easier to forgive him because he held me afterward.

My eyes narrow. "What does that have to do with anything?"

"Because I haven't been able to stop thinking about it. What happened to you?"

I sigh. "Some guy picked me up and tried to kill me."

His free hand trails up my inner thigh. "That wasn't all he did. What did he do to you?"

I drop my gaze, shame brewing inside me. Somehow, I'm always the one left feeling the shame and guilt while the rapists get to go about their everyday life like nothing happened. How can their actions destroy me while simultaneously having so little effect on them?

"He raped me."

When I meet his eyes again, they flicker with anger. A harsh breath leaves his lips, and his grip tightens on my inner thigh. He leans down, getting close to my ear. "I wanted to lick you clean that night, bones. Make you forget it all happened."

His words send a shiver through my core. This dude literally thinks he can lick away anything and make it all better. He has no idea just how broken I am. How fucked up I am.

70

He lowers his hands and places Van Gogh in my waiting palms. I clutch the ragged squirrel to my chest, grateful my comfort object has been returned with no further damage.

"Thanks," I say. I turn my eyes back to Dalton. "I still don't understand why you wanted to know what happened to me. We can't do anything about it. The police will view me as just another junkie." I carry Van Gogh to the dresser and put him back in his rightful place. "Besides," I say with a sigh, "it's not like we could find that guy again, and there are about a million others just like him. You saw that for yourself today."

Dalton's eyes slide to the side, and I can see the wheels turning in his mind. "We can't punish the man who did that to you, but maybe we can get our own version of revenge," he finally says.

My eyes harden on him. "What do you mean?"

"It's Halloween tonight."

I cock my head. "And?"

"Let's do a Halloween spree," he says, his eyes lighting up with a devilish gleam.

"Like . . . a killing spree?" I laugh. "Who do you think we are?"

Dalton shrugs. "Weirdos. Creeps. Freaks."

A smile crosses my lips. He's not wrong there. Instead of feeling offended, I feel almost exhilarated to find someone else who understands what it's like to be an outsider. I haven't exactly toyed with murderous thoughts before—not seriously, anyway—but his idea sparks something in my brain. He's just held a match to a dormant fuse inside me, and I wouldn't mind leaving a little destruction in my wake when I detonate.

I pull out of his grasp and go to my closet. The hinges

squeal as I pull open the door, then I remove two black masks from the shadowy recesses of the top shelf. A large purple X slashes across each eye, and the mouths have been sewn shut with thick black twine. They're the children born of a marriage between terrifying and cute. I picked them up a few weeks ago because I figured I would need them while I got up to some solo bullshit during a raging drug-induced high, and I grabbed two because I knew I'd likely lose one during some wild adventures. But this is even better. It's almost kismet.

I pull the elastic band from my ponytail and put on a mask before handing the second one to Dalton. Without any hesitation, he puts it on. My panties literally dissolve when I see the tall, brooding, terrifying man before me. The mask only adds to the imagery, and when he grabs the baseball bat I keep behind the door and spins it at his side, he transforms into my perfect monster.

New kink unlocked?

He walks over to me and yanks down my jeans without even unbuttoning them, then he drops to his knees and raises his mask just enough to expose his mouth. He buries his face between my legs, the plastic crinkling as he tastes me. I reach over, grip the dresser, and grind my clit against the mask as he licks me. The bat falls to his side before his hands ride up my thighs and grip my ass.

"Ride my face, bones. Come on my mask," he growls.

With each long stroke of his tongue, he drinks more of the wetness that gathered between my legs while I sucked his cock in the bathroom. When he spit blood in my mouth, I nearly came myself. I didn't think I'd like to be spit on, and I certainly didn't know the blood would only add to the moment, but here we are, finding all sorts of new kinks today.

Don't Stop

The sensations electrify me—his rumbling voice, the warmth of his tongue, those big purple X's staring up at me as it curves around the top of his head. I bury my hand in his hair and grind myself over his soft mouth and the hard plastic mask.

"I'm coming," I pant, tilting my pelvis so he can get a better angle. "Don't stop."

I can almost feel him smirking against my pussy as he licks my clit with a methodical quickness that turns my body to liquid. He handles my pleasure the same way he handles his work—fucking perfection in every stroke—and I gush on the mask and his chin. He pulls away from me and stands, lowering the mask so I see my creamy wetness on the black plastic.

He leans into me. "Lick it. Clean me," he growls.

I grip both sides of his head, pull him into me, and drag my tongue from the bottom to the top of his mask.

"Good girl, bones. Now get your shit together. We're getting out of here."

"Where are we going?"

He raises the mask, and his hungry eyes flame, heating me to my core. "On a road trip," he says, his voice low and gravelly.

"I can't go," I say, the excitement deflating from my body. "I still have a few days left in the house. If I leave early, they'll take out a warrant for my arrest."

"It's one night, bones," he says. "I'll have you back by morning. No one will even realize you're missing, especially since this place doesn't exactly do bed checks."

It's not a terrible idea, but I'm not sure we can sneak past the front desk. "If Lucy sees me leave—"

He silences me by motioning to the window. "That's how I got in here last night. No cameras. No sensors.

They've probably made you believe this place is Fort Knox at night, but they lied."

I bite my lower lip and look from Dalton to the window. The half-baked plan to go on a murder spree for Halloween seemed like a good idea a few minutes ago, but now that the pleasure-fueled haze has cleared from my mind, I'm not sure this is a risk I'm willing to take. I've endured this shitty program for weeks, and I'm so close to being free from the cage. Getting caught after hours—or getting caught while committing a fucking homicide—means returning to jail.

Sensing my indecision, Dalton steps closer. He raises my mask and looks into my eyes, then lowers his voice to a whisper. "What do you want to do?"

What I want to do and what I should do are two very different things, but when I stare into his icy gaze, I have my answer.

Chapter Eleven

Dalton

She stuffs a few changes of clothes and a pair of gloves into her backpack. We'll only be out for one night, but the clothes are a smart idea since it will be hard to find victims if we're covered in blood. Then again, it is Halloween. The fucked-up little squirrel peeks from a mesh water bottle pocket. Does she really just leave it on display like that? She's so fucking weird. But why does her weirdness attract mine? Why does she make me want to explore my sexual side? The thought of fucking her while she's awake both intrigues and disgusts me. I don't want her to judge me, but I also can't deny my urge to feel her around me. At least I know I can please her with my mouth if I suck at the fucking part.

We ease out of the window and head for my SUV, careful to stick to the shadows. She slides into the passenger seat and tucks the bat beside her. I slip the key into the ignition. I worry it won't start as it emits a pathetic symphony of sputters and squeaking belts, but it finally catches and roars to life. She side-eyes me. It's not the ideal car for a road trip, I guess, but it's all we've got.

I stop by my house before we head out on our mission. She doesn't ask to come inside, which I'm glad about. I don't want her to see how I live. Instead of the strewn clothes and mess of a typical bachelor pad, it's all clean lines and simplicity, just the way I like it. Well, the way my OCD likes it. She already knows I'm obsessive, but I'm not ready to show her the extent of my need for order.

I grab an old backpack from my closet and shove several knives and a pair of gloves inside it. It takes every ounce of my willpower to resist the urge to fold the clothes into neat squares, but we don't have time for that. On my way out the door, I stop by my junk drawer and grab the duct tape. Just in case. I return to the car and get inside. She's rolled down the windows, probably to air out the constant scent of paint that clings to the upholstery. Autumn wind blows through the open windows and chills me.

Without speaking, we make our way down the road.

"So what's the plan?" she asks, breaking the silence with her soft voice.

I grip the steering wheel. I hadn't thought that far through this. When I heard what happened to her, it made me so angry that I conjured up the road trip of homicide on the spot. I didn't even think she'd go with it, but she pulled out the masks with such a big smile on her face, and that solidified everything.

I clear my throat and turn onto a side road. "We'll drive out of town, pick up hitchhikers . . . and kill them."

She nods. If she's second-guessing what we've decided to do, she doesn't show it. Her eyes focus on the lines in the road as they disappear beneath the front of the car. I'm second-guessing it, but when I think of what those men put her through, it renews my will to unleash this side of myself. The side that has been lurking in the recesses of my mind since I was a child. This woman has flung the door wide and set it free.

After an hour of small talk and traveling along deserted back roads, the smell of burning rubber drifts through the open window, carried on the wind blowing into the car. The temperature gauge tips toward the red. That's really not good, but I don't say anything. I don't want to alarm her or risk ruining our fun-filled plans. A sign for a campground appears, and I get an idea.

"Let's pull into this campground and stay until later tonight," I say. I'm worried this shitty car will cut our road trip short, but maybe we can salvage the evening if we let it cool down.

I steer the car toward the campground's deserted entrance. Since it's postseason, I don't expect to see anyone at all, but a group of people waits just inside the woods. They've clearly gathered here to party for Halloween, and they probably brought plenty of drugs and alcohol—the things I would like to keep Rayna from. Regret fills me, and I consider turning around. Instead, I pull into a campsite and ignore the music blasting from nearby.

We get out of the car and put on our jackets, and she gravitates toward the noise like a moth to a toxic fucking flame.

"Bones?" I say.

She stops and turns toward me.

"No drugs."

"We're going to commit homicides, and you're worried about some drugs?"

Fair, but still. "No. Drugs."

"Party pooper," she says, sticking her middle finger up at me.

I sigh, grab the masks, put a knife in my pocket, and follow her. It doesn't take long to reach the campers. Their rising bonfire sends a flicker of orange between the leafless trees. Laughter and music vibrate my ears. A camper sits in a large RV spot, the fire blazing in the pit beside it. People mill around the fire and the tables dotting the campsite, and everyone wears a costume.

I hand Rayna's mask to her and ready mine. We slip them over our heads, but we keep them pulled up. I'd rather stay back in my car and do *anything* else. I don't like socializing. Clearly, Rayna does. She's absorbed into the crowd like she knows everyone. I stuff my hands in my pocket, feeling uncomfortable with every step closer to the middle of the party.

A few beer kegs stand beside a table full of liquor bottles. A man hovers beside the table, taking long drags from a blunt. Rayna stops and stares at him, but she heads toward the alcohol after giving me a quick glance. I don't miss the look of longing on her face, but I'm glad she had the willpower to bypass the drugs.

She returns to me a few minutes later with a Solo cup in each hand. "Liquid courage?" she asks.

I shake my head. I'm not really a drinker. I'm not really a doer of anything, to be honest. The only thing I want to become intoxicated by is Rayna's blood.

She shrugs and downs one drink, then she slides the empty cup beneath the full one and sips on what remains. "Can we kill one of them?" she asks. Her voice is a hushed whisper that only I can hear.

I hope.

I look around at the kids. Because that's what they are.

They're probably in college. The girls must be freezing in their slutty Halloween outfits, and how they can stand the cold for the sake of male attention is beyond me. The guys look like a bunch of testosterone-laden shit heads. They're all obnoxious, but no. I don't want to kill innocents. I want to kill people who deserve it. People who would hurt her. People who would dare to touch *my* bones.

I shake my head. "Not here," I whisper.

She pouts and takes another sip of her drink. Her eyes keep darting to a baggie of cocaine on a book by the fire. Warm and inviting. I'm certain her mouth is watering for it. Probably the same way mine waters for her. When she steps away from me, I'm certain she's caving in to her baser desires, but she turns at the last second and goes for the table of booze instead.

My sigh of relief comes too soon, however, because when she reaches the table, the guy with the blunt has turned his attention toward her. He grabs a bottle, and she bats her eyelashes at him, a flirty expression on her face. With a coy grin, she holds out her cup and he fills it. She thanks the guy and his hand lingers on her arm. I bowl through the crowd to get to her, pushing the guy away until he's far enough for my comfort. I don't even want his eyes on her. She's *mine*.

"She was flirting with me, bro!" he hollers.

I ignore him and grab Rayna by the sleeve of her sweater, then pull her back toward the woods. "Did you have to flirt with him?"

She shrugs. "I was just trying to be friendly since we weren't exactly invited to this party and I was drinking his booze."

My jaw clenches, and I suck in a calming breath. "When I saw how he looked at you, I wanted to kill him. If we hadn't been in a crowd of people, I probably would have. Do you understand what that's like? To want to kill someone for doing nothing more than putting his eyes on something that belongs to you?"

She shrugs and downs the drink, leaving a little line of alcohol along the top of her upper lip. I swipe it away, and she grabs my wrist and pulls my thumb into her mouth. She sucks. The sensation of her tongue curling around my skin is enough to send me over the edge.

Yes, she's mine, and I need to remind her of that.

I grip her wrist and drag her through the trees. When we reach my car, I push her back against the cool metal. I pull my mask over my face, and her eyes focus on the big purple X's. My hand rises up the back of her thigh, and the other brushes her brown hair away from her beautiful face. Despite the cool bite in the air, the alcohol has warmed her skin. I long to feel more of her warmth. To taste her.

I reach down, unbutton her jeans, and begin to lower them, but she stops the descent. "Let me get a condom," she says.

I shake my head. "I've already fucked you raw, bones."

She stares at me, remembering her dream, I'm guessing. "You came inside me?"

"And cleaned you up with my tongue."

She pushes my chest. "Dick. What if I wasn't on birth control?"

"Then I guess I wouldn't be able to do this."

I spin her around and push her chest to the metal. With her pants still halfway down her thighs, I draw her ass toward me and work down my jeans. I spread the cuffs of her ass and push inside her. She gasps. I reach out and tug down her mask. I want us to remain faceless as we fuck.

People stumble through our site as they meander away

from the party, and while I can hardly see their faces through the bright X's over my eyes, I know they stop and stare. How could they not? It's a sight I wish I could bear witness to myself. Her perfect ass nestled against me as I pound into her. The masks help. It's easier to be brave with it on. Unmasked me would never let these losers watch. It gave me a new persona once I slipped it on. Confident. Cocky. Certain that I can fuck Rayna in front of them and make her come with their eyes on us.

I grip her shoulders for leverage so I can fuck her harder, and the soft moans she tried to hold back become screams. Her ponytail bounces with every driven thrust, and I don't think she's noticed our audience. Time to give them a real show. I reach around her and find her clit, rubbing her until her tone changes. The sounds drive the motion of my fingers, and she tightens around me.

"I'm coming," she pants, and I already know it. She's pulsating around me, her internal muscles rhythmically squeezing my cock. I rub her until those loud moans revert to whimpers, until the rhythm changes inside her. My eyes are drawn back to the people standing by and watching. I stare at them, and their enthralled gazes fill me with the need to fill Rayna. I finish deep inside her.

This mask gives me the confidence to fuck her. And hopefully it will provide the confidence to kill. The mask gives me the chance to be the *real* me for once. I have to go back to being the fallacy I've created once this night ends, but for now, I'm just me. This night has already started off better than I could have hoped. I can only imagine what waits for us down the road.

Chapter Twelve

Rayna

By the time we finish having sex, it's almost nine p.m. Distant voices and the thump of music drifts from the ongoing party as I walk into the bathroom across the road from Dalton's car. I expect the motion-sensor lights to flicker on when I open the door, but the interior remains dark. When I move to the sink, I work down my jeans and clean myself off the best I can with cold water. I turn around and press the paper towel dispenser's squeaky lever, but it only responds with an empty rolling sound. I wave my hand under the dryer, but it fails me as well. I return to Dalton, rubbing my wet hands down the front of my jeans.

"The paper towel dispenser was empty," I say. "The hand dryer and lights weren't powered either."

"It's the off-season. They probably turned shit off to save a few bucks."

"Well, at least there was water, even if it was cold." My

eyes move to the star-filled sky. "Do you think it's late enough to get back on the road?"

Dalton slides off the back bumper and gets into the driver's seat. As I join him in the car, the engine rumbles and rattles but doesn't turn over. Great. Our spree has ended before it even began.

"Son of a bitch!" he growls, slamming his hand on the wheel.

I stare at him. "What now?"

"I don't know." He inhales.

"We can take our backpacks and hitchhike."

His gray eyes leap to mine. "Someone may pick up your sexy ass, but they aren't picking up mine."

My hand wraps around my chin as I try to puzzle out a solution to this problem. "What if you hide? When someone pulls over, I'll tell the driver you're wasted and about to pass out, then I'll retrieve you from your hiding spot."

A light seems to click on above Dalton's head, excitement growing the longer he considers my plan. "And whoever tries to do something to you while I'm 'asleep' gets —" He swipes his fingers across his throat.

"Yes!" I squeal. "I love that idea! But what about the car?"

"We'll leave it here. We'll try it again when we're done, but if it doesn't turn over, we'll have to catch a bus back to town."

I nod, gather my bookbag, and throw it over my shoulder. I smile at Dalton. "Let's start walking."

M<small>Y BAT RESTS</small> at my feet. Wouldn't want to scare them off. With my thumb in the air and my mask perched atop my head, I watch as another car whizzes by. Like all the others before, it doesn't slow in the slightest. Dalton rustles in the brush behind me. He's probably sick of sitting there, even though it's only been twenty minutes since we chose our spot. I'm anxious too. We don't even know if our plan will work, and I'm ready to put it to the test.

Just as I'm about to head to Dalton and suggest we try a new spot, a car pulls over. A blond middle-aged man sits behind the wheel. He regards me with kind eyes as he flips on the dome light and lowers his window, and I'm even less sure this plan will work now. This man doesn't seem like the type to try anything weird with me.

Then again, they aren't always so obvious.

"You need a ride?" he asks.

"Actually, *we* do." I gesture toward the woods behind me. "My boyfriend is out there throwing up. We went to a Halloween party, and he got too drunk because he chose to pregame. We're just trying to get to a motel at the next exit so he can sleep it off." I lift my bat, and the man eyes it. "Just part of the costume," I say with a sweet smile.

The man nods, and I wave to Dalton. Like a practiced actor stepping onstage for his big scene, he stumbles out of the woods, wiping at his mouth before tugging his mask into place. He leans against the car and pretends to gag. The man roots around in the passenger seat before wiggling a plastic bag toward me. I don't blame him. Dalton is pretty convincing.

I open the back door to climb inside, but Dalton pushes my hand away. "Sit up front so I can lie down in the back."

I pretend I don't like that idea, but it was mine in the first place. We planned this detail down to the letter. I'm the bait, and I need to be as close as possible to the would-be monsters.

"You don't mind, sir?" I ask as I open the passenger-side door.

The man shakes his head and swipes a few empty Gatorade bottles from the seat to the floorboard. I sit down and Dalton gets in back and stretches across the seat. The mask hangs firmly over his face, but he's turned toward me so he can see everything. Minutes after the man has pulled onto the road, Dalton releases a soft hum of fake snores. Now we wait.

"What's your name?" I ask the man.

"Ervin," he says. "Yours?"

"Sally," I lie.

He makes a bit of small talk as we travel down the road, but his hands remain on the steering wheel and his eyes never leave my face when he glances at me, which isn't often. I haven't given up all hope for our first victim, though. I've been in enough cars to know that some of them like to play the long game. They'll wait until we reach the destination before demanding payment, and when I refuse, they'll take what they feel is owed to them.

Anticipation rises to a boil in my gut as we pull into the motel parking lot. Dalton keeps snoring, which is good. If the guy thinks he's passed out, he's less likely to worry about making a move.

He puts the car in park near the entrance and turns to me. "There you kids go," he says with a friendly smile.

That's it? He's not going to tell me to return the favor with my mouth or hand? He did this out of the kindness of his heart? I had grown bloodthirsty at the idea of having a kill with Dalton, and we're running out of time. It's almost ten o'clock, and I have to be back at Somerset House before they do wake-up calls at eight in the morning.

"You two be safe now," the man says when I don't move to get out of the car. The unexpected finality that cloaks his words evokes annoyance within me.

I get out of the passenger seat and whip open Dalton's door. His head falls back and he sits up. "Come on, Harry, we're here."

"Already?" he asks, trying to communicate with me without making it obvious.

"Yeah, I can't believe it either."

I help drag his fake drunk ass out of the car, and we wave off the nice fucking man who stopped for us. My adrenaline fades to a simmer as his taillights merge with the others on the road in front of the motel.

"What the fuck?" I say. "We still could have killed him."

Dalton shakes his head and takes my face in his hands. "I want to kill people with bad intentions, not good ones, and his intentions were disturbingly pure. If we're going to be killers, we have to have a code. We only kill people who deserve it."

Of course I'd go on a killing spree with someone with such a conscience. What if every car that stops is driven by a nice guy? Are we going to spare them all? What a kill block.

"Now what?" I ask as I stare at the road.

Dalton drags my mask over my face. "We try again. And again. We keep going until we find our target, then we make our kill, bones."

With only ten hours left, I'm not sure we'll ever accomplish our goal. But I'll be damned if we stop trying now.

Chapter Thirteen

Dalton

We walk a few miles down the road to a secluded area and put our plan in motion again. I stay in the woods near the road while her sexy ass tries to flag down each passing vehicle. An hour passes, but no one has so much as slowed down.

Rayna has removed the glove from one hand to make it more visible to passing cars. I play with the leather cuff of mine as I wait. Watching her work the side of the road, I can only think of how hungry she is for this kill. She wouldn't have cared one way or another if that man had or hadn't tried to sleep with her. She'd have happily still killed him. That's not how I want to do things. I want to kill people who would take something that doesn't belong to them before I take what doesn't belong to me either.

Their life.

Finally, another car pulls over. The man in the driver's seat talks to Rayna, but I can't hear what they say. She gestures toward me, just as she did with the first guy, and before her mouth even finishes moving, the car speeds off. Rayna's shoulders drop and a frustrated grumble rolls from her throat. She stomps her foot before throwing her thumb into the air once more. She's got a lot of determination. I'll give her that.

Ten minutes later, a pickup truck pulls onto the shoulder, and she starts her spiel again. This guy doesn't speed off when she motions toward me in the woods, and Rayna gives the signal for me to join her. I stumble out of the shadows like I don't know how to use my legs, bumping into a tree trunk for good measure. When I make it across the grass, I fall into her arms.

"He's so drunk. I'm sorry. He'll just pass out in the back." She slides her bare fingers into the second glove before opening the back door of the cab and helping me inside. I curl up on my side, keeping my head angled so I can watch out for her. The heavy metal slams as she gets into the passenger seat.

"Where to?" the squat man asks her.

"Just to the next exit. We're staying at a motel right off the main road."

I start snoring once I feel the tires roll onto the pavement. Nearly the moment I pretend to be asleep, he's creeping on her.

"You're too pretty to get stuck with a drunk little boy like that." He tosses his thumb my way, but I keep snoring. "Real men know how to handle their liquor. Have you ever been with a real man?" His hand lands on her shoulder, and she shrugs it away.

"No," she whispers.

"I could take you to my place. It's right off the next exit too. While your little boyfriend sleeps it off in the back, I could take you inside and show you how a real man can drink. And fuck."

His words inflame me. I hate every disgusting thing leaving his mouth. It's not sexy. It's foul. He's the definition of a cringe lord.

"Um . . . no thanks," Rayna says. "Our motel is fine."

The creep doesn't say anything for a little while, but something tells me he isn't done. The way he keeps licking his lips and staring at Rayna's chest, I can almost hear what he's thinking, and none of it bodes well for him. I'm glad we've waited for the right target. This douchebag will be an absolute joy to murder.

He turns off at the next exit, but instead of heading into town, he pulls onto a secluded side road and hides his fuckboy truck behind a wall of trees. He locks the doors, and the audible click makes my heart stutter against the wall of my chest. Before he can cut the engine, I reach into my bag and pull out a knife. If I'd waited until he silenced his look-at-me pipes, he'd have heard my gloved hand digging around in the nylon bag. I grip the handle in a tight fist and wait.

He pulls the keys from the ignition and leans into Rayna.

"No," she says, pushing against him, but he doesn't listen. "Please stop."

He ignores her and moves closer. As his hand moves toward her thigh, I sit up. He's too close to touching what's mine, and now I'm properly homicidal. I stab the knife into the side of his neck, and a wet, squelching sound breaks the silence. Rayna doesn't scream or look scared. Her gray eyes sear the man with unbroken focus as he wordlessly reaches for the handle sticking out of his neck. She flips her mask over her face and gets out of the truck. I follow her.

"Hand me the tape!" she says as she rounds the truck and whips open his door.

I toss the duct tape to her, and she wraps it around his bloody wrists so he can't get to his neck. Not that it would matter at this point. If he pulls the knife out of his flesh, he'll only die faster.

She tugs at his shoulder. "Help me get the fucker out."

I push her aside and do the grunt work of pulling him out and propping him against the hood of the truck.

"Wh-Why?" he asks, spitting blood down his chin.

"Because she said no and you didn't listen." I rip another piece of tape from the roll and shove it over his mouth.

I turn toward Rayna. The thick gush of crimson pouring from fuckboy's neck has hardened me, and I need her to ease the ache between my legs. I pull her into me. The broad, fake smile on the plastic face of my mask can't encompass how I truly feel. How stabbing him felt like something I've needed for so long. Forever.

"Pull down those pants for me, bones," I growl as I walk her into his truck. I have too much blood on my hands, and I don't want her to look unapproachable by covering her clothes in it.

The tremor of his body right beside me goes straight to my dick. She kicks off her shoes, puts her gloved hands into her waistband, and lowers her pants.

"Unzip me and pull me out," I say.

She does as she's told, all while those big purple X's look up at me. She pulls me out, and her leather clad fingers graze me. I put my bloody hand on her bare thigh and lift it.

"I'll show *you* how a real man fucks," I snarl toward the dying man. Snot froths and bubbles from his nose.

I hold the back of her thigh as I guide myself to her

opening and push inside her. She gasps as I drive her into the truck's metal.

"He's dying," she pants, her eyes falling to the man on the ground. "He's fucking dying because of us." Her hips curl, and she fucks me as much as I fuck her. Carnal, excited energy passes between us. Animalistic. Because we *are* animals, killing for fun. "I want to take the final stab. I want to be the one to kill him."

She clenches around me, loving every second of this sadistic moment. Living for it.

The energy sweeps through me, and I throw all caution to the wind. I lift her shirt and rest its edge on top of her perfect tits. Reaching down, I dip my fingers into the flow of blood oozing around the knife. So warm. So wet. So slick. My fingers move to her chest, and I paint her tits with slow, smooth, methodical lines. My fingers lift as I go over her peaked nipples, and the curves ruin my perfect lines.

"I'm the painter, and you're my fucking muse," I growl, squeezing her nipple between my gloved fingers. "You're a work of art, bones."

I drive my hips into hers, halting her movements with the strength behind each thrust. I reach down to gather more paint and wash the warm liquid across her stomach as I drop my hand between us. As soon as the warm, blood-coated leather touches her swollen clit, she twitches around me and her moans crest. She doesn't even tell me she's coming. I know because of the way she squeezes me. Her head drops back, and the mask muffles her moans of intense pleasure. I'm not ready to come yet, though. I wanted to get her off, and now that I've accomplished my mission, I pull out of her.

I wipe the blood onto her hips and help her into her pants. She keeps her shirt raised to let the blood dry on her stomach. The man's drowsy eyes widen at the delicious sight as she drops to her knees in front of him. Her tits draw together as she leans forward.

She rips off the tape covering his mouth. "I want to hear him beg," she says, dropping the rectangle of tape beside her.

"Please, please don't kill me," he pleads. His head tilts forward. His skin has gone ashen, and she's going to miss the opportunity to kill him if she's not careful.

"Do it. Kill him," I urge. I offer her a second knife, but she shakes her head.

She goes to the passenger side of the truck and pulls the bat from the floorboard. The mask covers her face, but I can almost feel her smile behind the plastic. As she steps over his legs and stands before him, the man raises his eyes to her. Like a typical piece of shit, he focuses on her tits before realizing what she holds at her side. Rayna raises the bat like she's about to swing for the fences, cocking it over her shoulder and tilting her masked head as she waits. Recognition dawns in the man's eyes, and his mouth opens in a shrill scream.

THWACK!

The bat comes around at lightning speed and connects with his skull, silencing him instantly. He slumps to the ground, his legs squirming beneath him. His body doesn't realize his brain is no longer working. Rayna raises the bat over her head and brings it down on his face with a peal of laughter. Blood splatters on the grass, and I nearly come in my jeans.

He finally stills, and everything goes quiet except for her crazed, panting breaths behind the thin veil of plastic. She turns to me and pulls the knife from my hand.

"What are you doing?" I ask.

"I want to see what he looks like inside."

Ah. Her taxidermy obsession. Of course she would. She'd love to get all up in there. Not me. I liked stabbing him and enjoyed the warm heat of his life force oozing from him, but I'm not as interested in the actual corpse. She wants to play in his body like it's a fucking amusement park, and who am I to stop her?

She works to cut him open, carving a straight line from his sternum to his groin. She struggles to part his rib cage and eventually gives up, opting to reach blindly into the hidden cavity instead. She finds what she's looking for and begins to tug with both hands until it comes free. When her gloved hand emerges, she's holding a bloody hunk of meat and muscle that looks almost like a delicacy.

His heart.

She holds it up to me, and I take it with a gloved hand. I bring it to my face and inhale the strong, metallic scent. Blood drips from the organ. I raise the mask and hold the heart to my lips, unable to fight the urge to taste it. I can't help myself, and Rayna is already back to working on her little project, so it's not like she'll notice. My tongue presses against the warm, tough muscle, and I lick it with the same reverence I had when tasting Rayna's pussy. Now that I licked it, it's mine, unfortunately. I can't leave it with the rest of him. As I watch Rayna work, I suck and release the tendrils of connective tissue hanging from the organ. It comforts me.

Rayna raises her mask as well, and wet, sloshy sounds fill the dark silence as she draws out his organs and entrails like she's pulling clothes from a suitcase. She seems so satisfied as she rubs the different textures through her hands, even through the gloves. She's so caught up in her work that she doesn't speak.

"I want to stuff him," she says as she looks up at me.

A bit of connective tissue that still clings to the heart falls from my mouth, but she doesn't seem fazed. Either she didn't see what I was doing, or she doesn't care. "With what?"

She looks around before rising to her feet and rushing into the woods. She returns with wet leaves and foliage from the ground. She goes over to the now empty cavity and starts . . . well . . . stuffing him. She repeats this process until his hollowed body is almost puffy.

She holds the flaps of his abdomen together. "I wish I had a needle and thread."

I take the duct tape from my pocket. "Would this help?"

She nods, and I hand it to her. Winded with excitement, she tapes the flaps together. She's so beautiful beside the ultimate destruction she's created. She stands up and looks down at her little project. The smile on her face shows a satisfaction I can't even begin to understand because I didn't complete the kill. Next time I will, and I'll wear that same shit-eating grin when I do.

Rayna turns back to me, and her eyes fall to the heart in my hand. "I saw you lick it," she says. "You don't have to stop."

Odd embarrassment overcomes me, flushing my cheeks, but she steps into me, takes the heart, and works down my pants. I'm still hard from fucking her earlier, and having my mouth around this organ only fueled my need. I don't know what she has planned, but I'm more than happy to let her take the lead.

Her gray eyes bore into mine as she rubs the heart against my dick. She pulls it away and, using the knife, cuts through the top of the organ before sliding it over my length.

Don't Stop

Her hand moves back and forth, fucking me with the human heart.

"Fill it," she moans.

I thrust forward, tearing the soft flesh as more blood spills over my dick. A deep groan rolls from my throat because it's pretty much everything I imagined. I used to put red paint on my cock and pretend it was blood instead of chemicals and latex. The real thing is so much better. When I thrust deeper, my balls tighten and I know I'm going to come. I moan, and she bites her lip. She's insane, but she's my kind of insane.

If licking it makes it mine, fucking it like this makes it ours. What the fuck will I do with a come-filled heart?

Burn it, I guess. Burn all of this while we plan our next move. The night is still young.

Chapter Fourteen

Rayna

Chilly water embraces my body as I dive into a pool in some stranger's backyard. The lights are off in the house, keeping the backyard blanketed in darkness aside from the pool lights. A splash disrupts the water as Dalton jumps in after me. We needed a way to clean up after our first kill because we don't want it to be our last. Counting the time it will take to drive back to Somerset House, we still have seven hours to find another victim. Maybe more.

The blood vacates our skin, blending with the large volume of water around us. Our masks and clothing sit on the edge of the pool. We'll have to ditch those outfits. We can tell people the blood is fake and goes with our costumes, but there's no denying the strong metallic smell of the real thing. Thankfully, we were both smart enough to bring something to change into.

Dalton pops up beside me. His naked body presses against mine as he pulls me into him. My breasts peek above the waterline and goosebumps pebble my exposed skin. It's warmer inside the water than it is outside. He brushes my wet hair from my face. "You did so well. You were so fucking good."

My cheeks flush as his praise warms me from the inside out. I loved playing in that man's body and exploring it with the innocent curiosity of a child. The different textures and shapes. The weight of each organ in the palm of my gloved hand. It felt so wrong and taboo. I walk around with all of these same pieces and parts inside my body, but I've never gotten to see them or hold them. Now I have, and I loved every second of it.

"I loved watching you and seeing how happy you were," he says.

I blink at him. "But did you like doing what we did? Baiting and killing a man?"

He leans in and his lips brush against mine. He smirks. "I came inside a heart for you, did I not?"

Fair. He was rock hard the whole time, and only someone who enjoyed the act could have been so aroused by it.

I close the gap and kiss him, only pulling away to catch my breath. "You get the next kill."

THE OVERPOWERING SCENT of chlorine clings to our skin and fills the enclosed space of a stranger's SUV. It smells like we were actually at a Halloween party instead of bathing away the blood and changing our clothes. Dalton "snores" in the backseat, and I'm shocked by how much faster we found our victim this time.

Don't Stop

The man who picked us up appears younger than the last. Better looking than the last too. The sick, sadistic part of me hopes he'll try something because his body will be fun to explore. I want to find differences and compare organs. And he doesn't disappoint me. Instead of listening to the directions I gave him, he turns onto a utility road. Excitement and fear swirl inside me.

"Where are we going?" I ask, leaning forward to look around the dark, unpaved road.

"Thought we could pull over and have a drink. Your boyfriend seems like he's had enough, though." He looks back to make sure Dalton is still asleep, then he throws the SUV in park and flips on the dome light. He reaches back, digging around in front of Dalton. He pulls a beer from a case on the floorboard and hands it to me.

"I don't know," I whisper, looking down at the drink.

"Come on, it's just one drink."

I reach out and accept it, and we share the drinks in a stale silence. A raging hard-on tents the crotch of his jeans, and he makes no effort to hide it. Finally he lowers the window, crumples the can in his fist, and drops it outside. So he's a creep and a litterer. Gross.

He leans into me. "What's your name?" His fingers trail up my thigh, and my skin crawls.

"Sally," I say. I'm not sure why I lie again. He won't live long enough to give my real name to anyone. I try to pull my thigh away from his touch, but he sinks his fingertips into my flesh and holds me in place.

"Well, Sally, I'm Luke. No need to be nervous with me. I'll take care of you." He leans closer, and his hot breath grazes my cheek.

Panic crawls up my throat, and I pull backward. "No, I don't want to do that," I say. "Please stop."

His gaze hardens. "You made me give you a ride, and you drank my beer. It's the least you can do," he says, a sharp rise in his tone. He looks back at Dalton to see if he woke him up. Satisfied my partner is still asleep, he leans closer again and his lips land on the side of my neck.

"Stop!" I tell him, raising my voice.

It doesn't matter. His relentless lips find mine, muffling my protest.

Wake the fuck up, Dalton! I scream in my head.

The man jerks away from me, his back pressed against his seat as his legs scramble in the footwell. His hands rise to his neck, and I realize why he's pinned to the seat. Dalton has wound a shoelace around his hands and looped it around Luke's neck. His fingers try to get beneath the thin, black shoelace, but it's useless. It's too taut. Blood collects on his fingertips as he scrapes his skin with each desperate attempt to gain enough room to draw a breath. Above the ligature, his face reddens like a tomato, then shifts to a bluish-purple. He claws at Dalton's wrists, but they're covered by his jacket.

The beautiful struggle between the two men turns me on. The man's will to live. Dalton's show of strength to ensure he doesn't. They merge into the perfect form of fore-play. I ache between my legs over it, and by the time the man stops fighting and his limbs grow flaccid, I'm throbbing and blind with arousal.

"What do you want to do with him, bones?" Dalton asks.

He doesn't want to know what I want to do to him. I don't even know if I have the courage to admit it to myself. "I want him against the car like the last guy."

We drag the man from the driver's side and set his life-less body against the panel of his dark SUV. We leave the driver's side door open so the dome light can illuminate us a bit. It's just enough to set the mood.

I stare at the handsome dead man. My eyes rove downward, and I notice his wicked case of angel lust. My thoughts go to very immoral places, but it's not like I have very far to fall from grace. We just murdered him, and you can't get much more immoral than that. But I can try.

I drop to my knees beside him and rip open his jeans to reveal his post-death erection. He's not long or very thick. It's nothing special at all, except for the fact that this hard dick is attached to a dead man.

And that excites me.

"What are you doing?" Dalton asks, a hint of possessive jealousy in his question.

I bite my lip, afraid to say what I'm thinking of doing. Then again, he blew his load inside a human heart, so he's not exactly in any position to judge me. "What if I want you both inside me? What would you say to that?"

Dalton's mouth drops open, and I worry his jaw will unhinge and hit the ground. Fair response, to be honest. It's one thing to kill a man, but to fuck him after?

"What? No. I don't want another man inside you," he says.

I look down at him. "He's not a man, Dalton. He's a corpse. No different from fucking a doll. There's nothing in his head. Nothing in his chest. Just something between his legs."

Dalton's fists clench. "Bones . . ."

"I want a threesome with both of you." I clasp my hands together and poke out my lower lip. "Please?"

He closes his mouth and runs his hand through his hair as he looks between me and the corpse. His mouth works, but he can't form any words. As his shoulders slump and his hands fall to his sides, I know his resolve is weakening. I motion him toward me, and he comes. I point toward his jeans, and he undoes them. He pulls out his cock, and I lean forward and take him into my mouth. While I'm sucking him, I lean down and stroke the dead man's cock with my gloved hand. I moan at the feeling of my mouth and hand filled with dicks. When I remember that one of them is attached to a dead guy, a rush of heat barrels through me.

"One rule," Dalton says.

"Anything," I tell him, rolling my eyes up to his face.

His eyes focus on my hand as it works the man's length. "You have to use a condom with him. He doesn't deserve to feel your body raw, even if he's dead."

The excitement nearly makes me scream. I release my grip, rush to my backpack, and grab one of the condoms I keep on hand in case I need to do something unsavory for a hit. My eyes remain on Dalton as I go back to the body and squat beside it. I rip open the package and pull out the clear rubber. My pussy drips with anticipation as I roll it over his dick, which is a lot harder to do while wearing gloves.

I stand up and strip off my shoes and jeans. The condom is lubed, which is good. What I'm about to do will require a little help. Facing Dalton, I stand with one foot on either side of the dead man's lap. "Are you sure?" I ask. I'm giving him an out, but I don't want him to take it. I want to feel this dead thing inside me.

Dalton nods and wraps a gloved hand around his cock. Butterflies dance in my stomach as I squat and line up the cock with my ass. I lower myself and ease his dead dick into my ass. Pain sears through me as he stretches me, and I suck in a sharp breath. I lean back and rest on his motionless chest. His motionless everything. I grab his lifeless hand and put it on my inner thigh. I want him to touch me.

Don't Stop

Dalton's hand speeds up on his cock, matching my motions as I begin to move on the man's lap. I need him. Need his warm, breathing body to counteract the cold, lifeless one beneath me. He walks over, kneels in front of me and straddles the man too. The angle isn't great, but it's doable. Dalton inches closer and puts his cock up to my vacant opening. He pushes the head of his dick inside me and I gasp. He can't thrust deep at this angle, but despite that, I feel so full. So alive. Unlike the man in my ass.

I move my hips, riding both dicks, and my moans aren't the least bit controllable. My lower lip relaxes as I let the pleasure roar through the night air. Dalton puts his hands on the metal behind us and increases the tempo in his thrusts.

"Do you like that dead man's cock in your ass?" Dalton asks, his voice low and gravelly.

"I like it," I pant, "but I fucking love that I have both life *and* death inside me. I love that you're fucking me too, Dalton." A moan rolls out of me.

The man beneath me is motionless like a doll, yet soft and fleshy like a human. That's where death differs. Where it's similar.

Dalton reaches between us and rubs my clit. It's a pulse of electricity when I already feel so electrified. I'm giving in to a compulsion I never thought was possible. His touch just adds to it. How fucked up is it to kill a man, then come on his dick?

Fuck.

I clench around Dalton at the thought, and he groans. His touch brings me closer and closer until I'm coming around them. Pleasure wracks every inch of my body, and the full feeling only adds to it. It bursts through me like fucking fireworks.

The dead man can't come, but Dalton can, and I want him to fill me. "Come for me," I tell him.

"Anything for you, bones." He looks behind me at the man. "Literally, anything."

I smirk and his hips stutter against me. He pulls out of me and puts his cock away to prevent any spillage, but he surprises me when he gets as low as he can and puts his warm tongue between my lips. He laps up his come, giving extra attention to my clit with every stroke of his tongue. He cleans me up so nothing can drip from me and be left behind. Fuck, it feels so good that I wonder if I've died and gone to heaven. Then I remember the dead man's dick buried in my ass, and heaven isn't where I would end up. I also don't think hell would feel *this* good. Nope, it's real life —my very own pleasure-soaked purgatory.

Dalton sits up and grabs my chin. "Open your mouth and take both of us," he growls. "We've committed enough sins so far, so taste one more."

I part my lips and stick out my tongue, and Dalton deposits the mixture into my mouth. I should hate the way he's standing over me and degrading me by spitting into my mouth, especially considering how quickly I'd punch anyone else in the dick if they tried this, but I happily take everything he gives me. I enjoy the taste of our pleasure.

Dalton strokes my cheek with the same hand he used to murder the man beneath me, yet I don't shy away from it. I don't fear him.

"Good girl, bones," he says.

I think I'm ready to give up the drugs for good. This man will be my new addiction. Somerset House tried their best to save me from myself, but all along I just needed someone to see me and accept these fucked-up pieces of my soul.

Don't Stop

Dalton pulls out his phone and checks the time. "I think we can manage one more before we head back," he says.

Those words send shards of glass through my chest. I don't want this night to end. I don't want my time with Dalton to end. But nothing lasts forever, I guess. Instead of asking the question burning through my mind, instead of asking if I'll ever see him again after this crazy night, I nod and begin to dress. I'll get an answer one way or the other, but for now, we have one more victim to find.

Chapter Fifteen

Dalton

We play our game again, setting another trap. Instead of a cage with a pussy waiting at the end of a pressure plate, we turn their car into their cage. We trap them inside with nowhere to go. I want this last kill to go a little differently, though. I want fear and suffering this time. Everyone died too quickly, and all the fun happened when they were already dead. That was fun, too, but I want a little more playtime and a lot more blood.

I knew Rayna liked dead things, but I never imagined she'd want to have a fucking threesome with one. We're a match made in hell and even the devil is blushing at what we've done. It's fine. It felt good, and she looked fucking ecstatic, and that's what matters. I like killing, but I clearly don't have the same sexual deviancy which possesses her. When their life force drains from their body, hers fills her clit.

A fancy sports car pulls up, and I hide behind a shed this time. My eyes lock on hers but the more I think about it, the more my muscles ache to leap out. What if the man just grabbed her and stuffed her into the car with him? I wouldn't be able to get to her in time. She'd be gone. That thought makes me more homicidal than I already am, but then I remember her knife in her boot and her dead fucking squirrel keeping watch from her bag. She'll be fine.

Rayna motions me over, and I stumble toward the car. I feel like I walk more like I have polio, but they seem to believe it.

"Sorry, he's wasted," she says. "He'll just fall asleep in the back as soon as he puts his head down."

I don't talk because I'm not good at sounding drunk either.

"He's not gonna throw up back there, is he?" the guy asks as I open the door and climb into the backseat.

I glance at the youthful face behind the wheel of the sporty black car. Mommy or daddy bought him this ride, I presume. He hardly looks old enough to have earned enough money to buy a car worth more than I could ever afford. Must be nice to have the love and support of your parents. Maybe I wouldn't be an obsessive-compulsive, homicidal psychopath if I'd had that same support. The irony is that their love could be the thing that gets their son killed. It's his car that will become his cage, after all.

I pretend to doze off, releasing uneven snores. The driver glances in his rearview mirror and turns up his shit rap music to drown out the racket. We should kill him for his taste in music, but that goes against the rules. I said I wouldn't kill people who didn't deserve it, even if they are tasteless.

I almost fall asleep to the smooth rumble of the nice fucking car. The luxury seats conform to my body, and the driver's bland personality and weak attempts at small talk lull me toward unconsciousness.

He laughs and thrusts a thumb my way. "I've gotten drunk like that myself a time or two."

When? You just left your mother's vagina last week. I stare at him through the holes in my mask.

"Harry usually holds his liquor better than this, but we *love* Halloween," Rayna says.

The driver offers a dry chuckle. "Harry, huh? What's your name?" he asks, the rise of a poorly performed flirt in his tone.

"Sally," Rayna says with a giggle.

The kid has no clue where she pulled the names from. He's too young to put two and two together. He wasn't even a dream in his daddy's balls when that movie came out.

"I'm Sean," he says, his eyes dropping to her chest. "You said the next exit, right?"

Rayna nods. Her eyes fall to something she wants, just as his did. She spots a roach in the cupholder.

"You wanna smoke?" he asks.

Rayna bites her lip and nods.

"We can't smoke in the car, though," he says, and I want to fucking slap him. He probably doesn't want to shatter Mommy and Daddy's illusion of their perfect little man. With a shit-eating grin, he pulls onto a secluded road. Perfect for smoking weed, I guess.

And murdering.

Rayna pulls a lighter from her backpack and takes the roach with her as she gets out of the car. She stops just outside Sean's door, and he looks back at me once more before getting out. He takes the roach from her hand, and the cherry glows as he lights it and inhales. Thick smoke blows from his mouth, then his attention seems to narrow in on her as the high takes over.

His courage rises, and he reaches out and tucks her hair behind her ear before running his hand down her arm. Each touch makes my blood boil, even though Rayna shrugs away from it. His arm winds around her waist, and her muscles stiffen. She doesn't like to be cornered, that's for sure, and I'm at a severe disadvantage here. I'll never understand why she thought it was a good idea to get out of the car with him, but there they are. He pulls her closer, and she works twice as hard to push him away.

He leans in for a forceful kiss, and her harsh whispers rise to a scream. I reach for the door handle, but blood splashes across the window before I can even get one foot on the ground. When I try to push open the door, something presses against it and keeps me inside. I throw my weight into it, and it finally flies open.

Sean slumps beside the door, clutching his neck. Dark red ribbons weave through his fingers. She slashed his throat with the pretty little knife in her hand. The whites of his eyes shine in the dark, and he opens and closes his mouth like a fish just hauled onto land. I look at Rayna, at the blood splashed across her skin like a work of living art, and I'm mesmerized. I've never seen something so beautiful and dangerous in my life.

She hands the knife to me, and I spin it in my grasp before squatting down next to the dying young man. This idiot has been cut down in his prime because he couldn't take no for an answer. Young guys are such entitled pricks these days. Well, I guess it's not just the young guys, since the grown-ass men acted that way too. They just drove shittier cars.

I lift the kid's shirt and dip the tip of the blade into his drawn-up abdomen. He's too weak from blood loss to try to wiggle away. Even if he could, the fear holds him in place. He's clamped firmly in the jaws of shock. I continue my work as he silently screams in my ear. I lift the blade away and sink it beneath his skin, again and again. When I'm done, I turn to Rayna and showcase my work.

I carved a smiling pumpkin face into his gut.

It's a little sloppy, I guess, but just because I paint doesn't mean I'm an artist. My lips draw into a playful smile. "It's gourd-geous," I say with a laugh.

Her smile matches mine as she steps closer to assess my work. I continue to torture him until his jaw begins to relax and his head falls forward. He hovers on the precipice of death, and I'm ready to shove him over the side. I cut off his ear, and *that's* the final straw. The last bit of fun wanes as his chest stills.

Unless you're Rayna, of course. She's looking at me like the fun is just beginning. As far as she's concerned, his final breath has just whispered across her slit. I had my fun, and now it's time for her to come up with some sadistic game to finish off the night strong.

A sadistic look crawls across her face. She walks over, rips the ear from my hand, and pockets it before grabbing the knife. She straddles Sean's lap and rips open his jeans.

"We're not having another threesome, bones," I tell her, flat out, because he's too fucking young—not young enough to stray into pervert territory, but young enough to make it weird.

"I don't want a threesome, Dalton," she says, straining as she pulls his jeans down a bit. Gross, squishy sounds emit from the area where her hands fuck around with something on his lap. Only once she sits back on her heels do I see what's in her hand.

It's his fucking dick.

At first I think she plans to fuck herself with it, which honestly doesn't horrify me as much as I thought it would. Instead, she bites her lip and starts disemboweling the thing. Disemboweling isn't the right word, but it's the right action. She's skinning it. The sound of whatever is inside my own dick hitting the ground twists my stomach out of principle. That's a sound no one should hear.

She turns to look at me, the flap of flaccid skin dangling from her fingers. "I want you to wear him," she says. The intensity in her eyes burns through me.

"Uh, what?" I ask, though I'm kind of afraid to fucking hear what she means. What she said is bad enough.

She stretches the skin between both hands. "I want you to fuck me with his dick. Wear his dick skin over your dick skin."

Yup, her explanation is way worse. *Way* worse.

I shake my head. "I'm not wearing another man's skin, bones." My voice is the definition of firm, unlike that dick in her hands.

She stands up and lowers her jeans to her knees. "Then just stuff it inside me or something. I *need* to feel it."

I'm unhinged as fuck, and yet she's disturbing *me*. That's a feat. I fucked a heart for her. Fucked a corpse with her. But I have to draw the line somewhere, and it's here. I won't wear a man's skin like fucking Buffalo Bill. She's elevated the level of fucked up to some uncharted terrain. Somewhere the devil himself refuses to venture into.

She rubs the skin along her slit, and when she bites her lips and moans, it makes my horrified cock spring to life. The more she pleases herself with that thing, the harder it is for me to keep my knees planted on the grass. I want to be the one to make her feel good.

Don't Stop

The line I drew begins to fade. She's a beautiful maestro of manipulation, I'll give her that, and she knows just how to make me do what she wants.

Fine, I'll wear the fucking thing.

I rise to my feet and step into her. Slowly, and with a disgusting level of eroticism, she slides the penis skin over my length like a macabre condom. I nearly come from the warm, gooey insides as they surround and squeeze me, and I fucking hate how much I'm enjoying this. I look down at the monstrosity between my legs. Even though the skin takes the shape of my penis, it sure as fuck doesn't look like mine. And it's *not* mine. I'm wearing someone else's fucking dick.

I turn Rayna around, because at this point, I guess I'm into flesh condoms. I lift my mask enough to let my lips drop to her neck, and she backs her ass into me. This girl is so greedy and hungry for me. And . . . it. I encircle the base of the frayed flesh with my hand and hold it against me as I push inside her. I *thought* the blood felt good around my dick, but now, with her heat squeezing me, I'm encapsulated in pure bliss. I can't believe I fought this. Even if it destined me to hell in the very next breath, I would shove this flappy dick skin in God's mouth if it meant I could experience this again. Worth it.

She's worth it.

This entire experience is.

I bring my free hand up to her throat as I thrust inside her. She reaches into her pocket and pulls out the ear. Her tongue slips from her mouth and she licks up the shell, finishing with a nibble of his earlobe. My lip curls in disgusted confusion because a strange arousal blooms inside me at the sight of her mouth on the ear I cut from the dead guy's body. She moans into it as she gets closer. She squeezes and tightens around me so hard that more blood

115

drips out the ends of the amputated sleeve. It reminds me of a cut toothpaste tube.

"Come for me, bones, with two dicks buried inside you." There's a whole new meaning to double vaginal penetration for me now. I didn't think I'd be into that, but here I am, my balls tightening at my own disgusting words.

She rides out her orgasm, then she stops moving against me. "Wait!" she says, and she catches me moments before I intended to rip off this skin and come inside her.

"What?" I ask as she takes a step forward and eases me . . . us . . . out of her.

"Come on my face," she pants. She drops to her knees before I can even respond. When she looks up at me with hungry, gray eyes, I can't help but give her what she wants.

I let my hand relax around my base as I go to strip away the skin, but she stops me. She grips me through him as she bites her lip. The skin sleeve stretches around my swollen head, and she increases the pleasure with every stroke of her hand. I wrap my hand in her hair and bring her closer to me. She opens her mouth, sticks out her tongue, and waits for me to paint her face.

"I'm going to come, bones. I want to coat your fucking lips," I growl.

A splash of blood-tinged come hits her cheek, and she turns her head to catch the next spurt in her mouth. Her eyes roll back in her head with pleasure brought about by nothing more than my secondhand come from a Franken-dick.

She releases me, and I try to calm my quick, ragged breaths so I can think clearly about this particular situation. I point toward the ear cradled in her palm. "What do you plan to do with that?"

She looks up at me, letting her tongue swipe her lips. "We can't exactly leave it, so I figured I could keep it."

"It's not a lost puppy. You don't get to take it home."

She pouts. "Serial killers keep trophies all the time."

"Yeah, and how does that turn out for them?" I snip.

"But . . . but Van Gogh doesn't have any ears." She shoots me a playful smirk.

I sigh. "Fine, you can keep the ear."

I would do anything for her. Truly. But now we have to get her home.

The thought of leaving her at that halfway house sends a bullet of regret through my gut. Even though death surrounds her, I've *never* felt more understood. Surrounded by utter death and destruction, I've never felt as alive as I do with her. I'm not ready to let this feeling go.

WE WALKED BACK to the campground, which was only a few miles from our last kill. With a little coaxing, I got my piece of shit car to start. It's on its last legs, but it gets us back home. I pull into the parking lot of Somerset House just as the sun turns the sky a gray hue. Like our eyes.

"Thanks for everything," she says as she gathers her things. "That was a really nice first date."

"Does that mean I can see you again?" I ask.

She shrugs her shoulders and turns to me. "That depends. I'll get out of here in three days, and I could use a ride."

"Haven't learned your lesson about hitchhiking?"

A smile parts her perfect lips. "Nope."

As she leans closer to kiss me, I catch a whiff of blood.

In the dark, we missed a small splatter of red against her cheek. I raise my thumb and pull the thickened glob away from her skin, then ease it into my mouth. I have no reason to hide my secrets around this woman. For once in my life, I can just be me.

Before I can swallow the metallic taste, she pulls my lips to hers and finds the blood with her tongue. As we did multiple times last night, we share the reward between us.

Yeah. I think I'll see her again.

Epilogue

Rayna

"The string of homicides that shook the community this day last year are still fresh in our memories. Named the Halloween Harvester, the killer left a path of violence and unexplainable cruelty in his wake. We have no leads on the identity of the assailant or any way to know if he will continue his reign of terror this year. The police department has advised all locals to avoid picking up any individuals who try to flag you down on the side of the road. Don't stop—"

I click off the television and narrow my eyes at the black screen. "They just automatically assume it's a dude? What dude takes people's dicks?"

Dalton shrugs as he puts on his jacket. "I think Dahmer did."

I scoff. "We live in such a misogynistic society. Women can be serial killers too."

He comes up behind me, the crinkle of plastic caressing my neck as he moves my hair to the side. He lifts his mask, and his warm lips send a shiver up my spine as they brush my skin.

"Would you like me to call the police and let them know the Halloween Harvester is a duo that involves a woman?"

I release a soft laugh. "No, I guess not."

"Then let them believe their serial killer is one fucked-up man who disembowels people and takes their body parts with him."

He draws his lips away and turns his head toward the desk in our bedroom. My beautiful collection rests on top of it. Van Gogh takes the prized position, front and center, even though his eye has started to loosen from his aging body. Beside it stands a thin jar filled with clear liquid. An ear floats in its center—my second wet specimen, but the first I fixed myself.

Though I plan to collect a few more.

Dalton places my mask into my hands, and the purple X's stare back at me. The memories of that night flash in my mind as I rub a finger over the plastic. Each and every delicious murder left an ache inside us once Halloween was over. Like our first victim, we were left as a hollow thing stuffed with nothing but a painful desire to act on our most carnal urges. We've been good, but tonight is Halloween.

For one night a year, while everyone dresses up as someone else, we can be ourselves.

I clench my thighs together as Dalton fills our backpacks and gathers the weapons. The excitement is somehow overbearing yet still not enough. He eyes me, sensing my growing arousal, and drops the bag at his feet. With his knee, he pushes my legs apart as he runs his hand down my stomach and slides it into my jeans. He rubs me above my panties, teasing me through the soaked fabric. My favorite foreplay is watching Dalton kill, and those visions race through my mind now. The way his strong hand wraps around a knife handle or how his muscles flex as he strangles someone. The way he gives in to my sadistic sexual urges.

"Come for me, bones, and we'll go on another spree. As soon as your come soaks my hand, we can head toward an unsuspecting town and play all night."

"They shouldn't stop for me," I say as his fingers light me on fire.

"If they were smart, they wouldn't."

No, they shouldn't stop for me, but I want them to. I want to be the judge and jury for their crimes when I say no. And I want Dalton to be the executioner.

I grip his wrist, holding him against me. My moans rise, surrounded by all my favorite living and dead things. Right as I reach my edge, I look into his eyes. "Don't fucking stop."

Make sure you check out the rest of Lauren Biel's hitchhiker romance standalones. These books can be read in any order. Please note: While the rest of the books in the Ride or Die series are very dark, they do not contain the same level of horror as *Don't Stop*.
Hitched: Books2read.com/Hitched
Along for the Ride: Books2read.com/MFMHitchhiker
Driving my Obsession: Books2read.com/
DrivingmyObsession

Connect with Lauren

Check out LaurenBiel.com to sign up for the newsletter and get VIP (free and first) access to Lauren's spicy novellas and other bonus content!

Join the group on Facebook to connect with other fans and to discuss the books with the author. Visit http://www.face book.com/groups/laurenbieltraumances for more!

Lauren is now on Patreon! Get access to even more content and sneak peeks at upcoming novels. Check it out at www. patreon.com/LaurenBielAuthor to learn more!

Acknowledgments

Thank you to my readers for making my hitchhiker books so successful. There will be more of them!

To my VIP gals (Lori, Kimberly, Jessie, Nikita, Lexi, Grace), I know you've been waiting impatiently for this story to come out. Thank you for being such a part of my life and my journey. Love you all.

Have you read *Butcher & Blackbird* by Brynne Weaver yet? Make sure you do. Her dark and twisty mind creates such incredible stories. I mean, great minds must think alike because we both thought the frankenpeen/meat sleeve was a great idea.

A big, huge round of applause for my husband, who is probably regretting who he married by this point.

Thank you to my valued Patrons. Your contribution helped make this book happen.

Lori (special love your way, friend), Michelle M, Tabitha F, Jessie S, Lindsey S, Erika M, Laura T, Kayla W, Venetta B, Jennifer S, Nicole M, Eugenia M, Nineette W, Savannah C, Kimberly B, Jessica C, BoneDaddyAshe, Diana W, Ashley T, Kimberly S, Sammie Rae, Sarah J, Stacy B, Kay S,

Allison B, Andrea J, Bethany R, Carla D, Chelle, Gabby S, Hollie P, Jennifer H, Jessica G, Juli D, Rebecca R, Samantha R, Sara S, XynideSuicide, @bethbetweenthepages, Sharee S, Janette S, Samantha W, Lourdes G, Kelli T, Kayla M, Erica W, and Victoria R

Also by Lauren Biel

To view Lauren Biel's complete list of books, visit: https://www.
amazon.com/Lauren-Biel/e/B09CQYDK87

Or

LaurenBiel.com

About the Author

Lauren Biel is the author of many dark romance books with several more titles in the works. When she's not working, she's writing. When she's not writing, she's spending time with her husband, her friends, or her pets. You might also find her on a horseback trail ride or sitting beside a waterfall in Upstate New York. When reading her work, expect the unexpected. To be the first to know about her upcoming titles, please visit www.LaurenBiel.com.

Printed in Great Britain
by Amazon